THE LOVER'S CHAIN

THE LOVER'S CHAIN

HEINOUS CRIMES UNIT™ BOOK THREE

DANIEL SCOTT

Published by Marlowe & Vane
an imprint of LMBPN Publishing
PMB 196, 2540 South Maryland Pkwy
Las Vegas, NV 89109

Previously Published as *The Lover*
Version 1.01, January 2023
ebook ISBN: 979-8-88541-372-5
Print ISBN: 979-8-88541-947-5

THE LOVER'S CHAIN TEAM

Thanks to our JIT Readers

John Ashmore
Jan Hunnicutt
Marty French
Daphne
Alison Kelly
Kelly O'Donnell

Editor

Natale Wynne-Morril

SEDUCTION

At least some part of Ted Hinson knew the difference between right and wrong, although he couldn't determine how large that part was. Two things were growing in him simultaneously: fear and confidence.

Neither had anything to do with right or wrong but rather rationality and delusion. He felt fear because he was too intelligent to believe this could go on forever. Sooner or later, he *would* get caught.

Warring with the fear was an increasing sense of confidence because he hadn't been caught *yet,* which Ted Hinson's rational mind would call delusion.

Ted was thirty-eight years old, and his reign of terror had begun two years ago.

While no single law enforcement entity knew it, five women had gone missing during this period at a precise clip of one every four months. It was now the twenty-fourth month in his reign and time for another to disappear.

Ted decided on one woman every four months because

of the *acclimation* process. It took four months to tame his lovers, or break them in, as one might a wild horse.

Sarah had been especially difficult, and Ted was still trying to understand if it was her age or her personality. She was pushing the limits of his patience, not to mention love, as well as his self-imposed four-month deadline. He thought that last night had been a major milestone in their relationship.

"You want to go to lunch with us?"

Ted looked up from his desk. Georgia Shingleton was at his office door. How long had she been standing there? His face showed no surprise, but he didn't like not knowing how long she'd been watching him.

"Not today. Have to catch up on some edits," he said.

"Okay. Want me to bring you anything back? We're heading to Raw Sushi."

"Mind bringing me a California Roll?"

"No, not at all," Georgia said. "See ya in a few."

"Thanks," Ted said and watched her leave. The California Roll wasn't for him, but Sarah. He'd bring it to her as a thank you. Perhaps even as a peace offering.

Ted looked at his open office door. Had she been there long, and if so, what had she seen? Him staring mindlessly at his desk?

He needed to stop concentrating so hard, especially at work. Or rather, he needed to concentrate on *his work* while here and leave his lovers for home.

Ted turned to his computer screen and moved his mouse, causing the light to flare on.

He would deal with Sarah tonight. Hopefully, she would take the sushi with a bit of grace. If not, he might need to do something harsh—something he never wanted for any of his lovers—but her four-month acclimation period was at an end, and it was time to bring another into the stable. He didn't have any more time for Sarah's antics.

The trip was already planned for this weekend. Come Monday, Sarah would need to obey. Ted took the oath of marriage very seriously, and there would be no divorce. Not for him or any of his wives. If they chose not to love him, then…

'Til death do us part.

Sarah Yields was twenty-nine years old when her abduction occurred. Since then, she'd turned thirty, although she didn't know it. Not for sure, anyway. In the beginning, she had tried counting the days by counting her sleep cycles, but that was quickly lost.

Sarah spent a long time thinking about how it happened. She had been so stupid, and if she ever got out of here, she would scream it to the high heavens. She didn't care about victim shaming or any other terms she had been taught to despise in college.

Sarah had been foolish, and while that wasn't the only reason she was here, it was at least one of them. The other reason—and most important—was that "Ted" was fucking insane.

Sarah thought these things to herself, but she was learning in perhaps the slowest and most painful way possible that she couldn't say them aloud.

Not if she wanted to avoid pain.

She'd been drinking entirely too much at a club, and she had thought the man older but intensely sexy. She'd quit listening to her friends' requests to come dance and paid no attention to their protests about going home with the man she had just met at the bar.

Alcohol and horny were a bad combination under normal circumstances, but when you combined those with a man named Ted, it turned into outright horror.

Sarah didn't remember much after leaving with Ted. She figured he must have slipped her a pill. When she woke, she was "at home," as Ted called it.

She sat in darkness. The other women here didn't talk. Sarah had spent many days trying to get them to. Ted's terror held them firm. They were all broken, just like he wanted. Sarah couldn't see the others in the darkness around her, but she heard them from time to time. Someone might let out a cry or a snore, depending on what they were doing.

Sometimes, a chain would rattle, the metal scraping across the concrete floor.

Sarah wasn't good with time anymore, but the women in the room seemed to share a sixth sense about when Ted returned. Their chains rattled more, and Sarah looked toward the stairs. Light would shine down, and a long shadow would be cast from the very top to where Sarah sat.

Ted's shadow. Her *husband*.

Last night had been bad. Sarah's tongue continually went to the holes in her gums. They hurt like hell, but the blood flow had finally stopped at some point during the night. Sarah knew it was crazy, but when she'd spat her teeth out, she had placed them neatly by her side.

Three of them. She couldn't see them, but she knew they were there. If she ever left here, she'd still have them.

It was hard to hear much of what went on upstairs. Sometimes Sarah thought she only hallucinated the things she did hear. Sitting in the mostly silent darkness caused the mind to play tricks. Something else she had learned since meeting Ted.

The door at the top of the stairs swung open. Sarah squinted against the pain the light caused, but she didn't want to miss anything that came next. If she were to have any chance of escape, she had to be alert. She had to see everything she could.

The shadow grew in size as Ted walked down the stairs. They never squeaked under his weight. The entire basement was a huge slab of concrete, which also muffled any noise his harem might make.

"Here, love," he said.

Ted stood in front of her. Sarah knew better than to try and stand, plus her muscles couldn't take it today. Last night's beating hadn't knocked her out, but it had been the roughest yet.

Ted squatted and placed a small Styrofoam box down in front of her. He opened it so that she could see inside.

"A California Roll. I wasn't sure what type of sushi you liked."

I'm going to kill you. I'm going to kill you, and if I ever look at another sushi roll again, I'll kill whoever brings it to me, Sarah thought. She didn't say anything out loud. She pulled the Styrofoam box back to her.

"Do you have anything to say?" Ted asked.

"Ssank oou," Sarah forced out, her swollen mouth not allowing her to form the sounds.

"You're welcome. I'm going away this weekend. Monday we'll have a new member of our family. I hope you'll treat her well, Sarah. I really do. I know how jealous you can be, and I know how mean that makes you. I hope you take some time this weekend to think about what you want out of our marriage."

I'm going to kill you. I'm going to kill you. I'm going to fucking kill you.

Sarah looked at the sushi, careful not to make eye contact while trying to see what was around her. It was always the same. There was nothing she could use to escape.

"Okay, then," Ted said.

He went through his ritual next. A disgusting thing that Sarah had learned well. He went from woman to woman, talking with each about his day. They never said anything in return.

He always kissed them and sometimes straight up made out, but so far he hadn't performed any hardcore sexual acts during *this* ritual. That came later, or at least Sarah assumed it did, although she hadn't yet been forced to take part.

Sarah listened to the psychopath talk to the other four women, speaking to them as if they were long-term lovers. He giggled, grew serious, petted them, and kept talking. Finally, when he finished his rounds, he climbed those concrete stairs again and went to make dinner.

Sarah was lucky. He had brought her dinner early.

CHAPTER TWO

"Do you feel therapy is helping any more, Christian?"

Had he known this question was coming? He must have because he didn't feel any real shock at hearing it, and *that* felt odd.

"No," Christian said. He stared at the picture behind Melissa, avoiding her stare as he always did.

"Why not?"

"I don't know. Maybe it's time for another therapist, another perspective," he said.

"Do you really think that's it, or are you saying that to hurt me?"

"I don't want to hurt you, Melissa," he said.

"Over the next week, I'd like you to think about what you want to get out of your sessions. I feel like you used to know, but now I'm not sure you care. Do you come here more to keep the routine going than any will to work on yourself?"

"To keep the routine going," he whispered.

"Time's up," Melissa said.

Christian exited his therapist's office. He walked outside and pulled a pack of cigarettes from his pocket. He didn't need to look up to know where the smoking area was. He'd been smoking for the past year and always had a cigarette after leaving a session with Melissa.

Other people stood underneath the "smoking tree," but Christian paid them no attention. He walked to the curb and looked out at the parking lot.

Fourteen months. That's how long it had taken for Melissa to come out and say it, if not in so many words.

Christian, I can't help you.

Christian took a drag on his cigarette.

Is that what you've been going for? Desperately wanting her to say it out loud so that you didn't have to scream it in her face? Congratulations, Christian. You succeeded.

Melissa wasn't the first person to give up on him, although she had outlasted Veronica Lopez.

She had called it quits two months ago. Her last phone call had come in at 4:58 in the afternoon. Christian had sent her to voicemail—for what turned out to be the last time.

Good for her, Christian thought. *She finally wised up.*

Veronica had been Christian's first girlfriend. His last as well, as far as he was concerned. To say his mother wasn't happy with his decision to end the relationship was probably an understatement. His mom was downright pissed, and she hadn't minced her words about it.

"This is the dumbest thing you've ever done, Christian. You're hurting this poor girl, and you'll never forgive yourself," she had said.

Now, Melissa was giving him his walking papers, too.

He knew she wouldn't term it that way, and neither would Veronica. They would probably say *he* gave them *their* walking papers. Maybe they'd be right. It depended on how you looked at it, he supposed.

He flicked the cigarette to the curb. There was a place to put the butts. Christian didn't so much as glance at it. He felt like dirtying the world.

"Luke and I are going to grab dinner. You want to come?"

Tommy waited for Christian to look up from his computer. He knew what the answer would be before the kid spoke.

Does the word "kid" describe him anymore? Tommy wondered. *Feels like the days of his youth are long gone.*

"No. Going to finish up here and head home," Christian said.

Tommy nodded but didn't leave the room. He looked at his partner a little longer. Christian didn't break eye contact.

"Have you talked to Veronica at all?"

Christian shook his head.

"Too bad. Alice said the six of us should go to dinner sometime." Had they ever been six? Tommy didn't think so. By the time Luke met his new girlfriend Riley, Veronica and Christian were pretty much done.

"Rain check," Christian said.

"Sure thing. I'll see ya on Monday. Give me a call if you're bored this weekend, all right?"

"Yup." Christian looked back to his monitor.

Tommy stared for a moment longer, then left his partner's office. He walked down the hallway. The sun was still out, which was a good thing. Tommy had spent the first twenty years of his working life rarely seeing the sunset because he spent his evenings in this building.

He hadn't done that for the past fourteen months. He tried to get out at five now, and while it had felt awkward at first, both he and his fiancée were glad he did.

Alice was busy with girlfriends tonight, so Tommy had made plans with Luke. He wasn't sure what Riley was doing, but Luke had been free. He could have asked Christian earlier in the week, but why make him come up with an excuse so far out? Christian wasn't coming to dinner, so there was no need to start lying days before.

"Ready?" Tommy asked, pausing at Luke's door.

"Yes."

Luke turned his computer off and grabbed his jacket. Tommy could still be taken aback by the ease with which Luke moved across the room. Even his movements were different than anyone else Tommy knew. He walked like a lithe cat. Smooth and elegant, with every muscle ready to spring if called upon.

"Steak?" Luke asked.

"Works for me."

The two of them headed downstairs to the parking deck. They took their own cars, which Tommy was grateful for. He wanted a bit more time to think about the Christian problem.

You couldn't see the scar that Lucy Speckle had left on his skull unless he parted his hair to show it—which Luke wouldn't do.

He hadn't spoken to Luke about the changes in their partner. He and Luke had last spoken about Christian in the hospital room fourteen months previously. Tommy had been trying to say Luke was wrong in forcing Christian to drive Lucy Speckle to suicide.

A chill had moved through Tommy in the hospital room, and it did now as he remembered Luke's words. It was the coldest Luke had ever been with him, and Tommy supposed that was why he had avoided discussing Christian's change.

He didn't want to feel that coldness again, as though a freezer filled the space where Luke's heart should have been, radiating intense cold out to the world.

"Jesus Christ, stop it," Tommy said to his otherwise empty car.

He had decided he would discuss Christian today and he didn't need to spook himself out of it. He and Luke needed to talk about their partner. Fourteen months ago, Tommy had been shocked and scared by what had happened. He no longer blamed Luke for the things he'd said to Christian. Now, he realized what Luke had said was necessary. If not, Lucy Speckle would have killed all of them inside that damn storage unit.

Luke had saved five lives, including Tommy's.

The cost had been Lucy Speckle's life and Christian's innocence.

Tommy parked his car at the restaurant and walked over to Luke, who was waiting at the new Tesla he'd bought six months ago.

"Could still smell Speckle's stench inside the other one," he had said. "Plus, the new model is better."

Another ninety thousand on a car. *Must be nice.*

The two walked inside the restaurant and ordered. Luke asked for a glass of wine and Tommy ordered a beer.

"You want to talk about Christian, don't you?" Luke asked after the waiter left.

"Yup." Tommy took a swig of his beer.

"It is concerning," Luke admitted.

"So you've noticed?" Tommy asked.

"How could I not? He seems intent on pushing everyone and everything out of his life. Everything besides work that is, and even you and I are being relegated to necessary evils. He needs us for his work, but wants nothing else to do with us."

Tommy nodded, glancing across the full restaurant. "That pretty much sums it up."

"You were right in the hospital. What I said to him, and consequently what it caused him to do, definitely had a serious impact."

"So what do we do?"

"I've been thinking about it."

Tommy looked at his partner. "Well, want to tell me what you came up with?"

"I called his therapist earlier this week. Without breaking patient confidentiality, she said she thinks the same. She's asked him to consider what he wants out of therapy because it's going nowhere right now."

"Plus he ditched Veronica after everything that happened. You're still her therapist, right?"

Luke nodded. He picked up his wine glass and breathed in deeply, swirled the dark liquid around, and breathed in again. He finally took a sip, closing his eyes as he did.

"How is she?"

"Well, at this point, she's doing better than Christian. He hurt her. Maybe more than Speckle did."

Veronica Lopez had gotten involved with the wrong group, as far as Tommy was concerned. The reporter had started by interviewing Luke about a project he'd worked on in his previous career. Since then, she'd been kidnapped by two separate serial killers. Both times because of her connection with Tommy's and Luke's FBI division.

She had, unfortunately, fallen in love with Christian. And now the kid—*Is that the right word?* Tommy's subconscious asked again—wanted nothing to do with her.

"That poor woman." Tommy shook his head. He looked across the table at Luke. "Look, we have to do something. He needs, like, an intervention."

Luke chuckled. "Those are reserved for addicts, but I understand your meaning. Give me a week or so and let me think about it."

Luke sat alone in his living room. The house was dark except for the lights shining in from his yard. The living room curtains were open, giving him an unobstructed view of the large lawn. His new car sat in the wraparound driveway. Luke paid no attention to it. He stared out of the window at the perfectly cut grass, but his mind was elsewhere.

Fourteen months had passed since Luke had forced Christian's hand in Lucy Speckle's storage unit. He had been planning such an action for some time, but the end result had surpassed even his expectations.

Their little group had solved three crimes in the past fourteen months, and Christian's work had been top-notch. Luke often wondered what the place Christian went when he made the incredible leaps that led to apprehending criminals looked like. At the beginning of Lucy Speckle's spree, Christian had grown scared of his internal mansion, but now Luke thought he might spend more time inside that mansion than he did in reality.

It must be a wondrous place, Luke thought.

Despite what Luke said to Tommy at dinner, he had no intentions of bringing Christian out of the cold place he had found himself in. Christian's life had never been a place of spring or had the warmth of summer. Christian's autism had made his life perpetual autumn, where things could be peaceful but the fear of winter was always around the corner.

Luke believed winter had finally beset Christian, bringing with it a freeze that no life could hope to spring from.

Unfortunately, Luke couldn't *force* Christian's continuing demise. The past fourteen months hadn't presented an opportunity for Luke to dive deeper into his psyche and push through the final barriers that were separating him from his fate.

A weird word, that. Fate. Especially given Luke's purpose in life.

Something would happen, Luke decided. Another opportunity would present itself, and when it did, he would ensure that the temperature surrounding Christian dropped below zero.

While Luke was sitting alone in his house at three in the morning, Christian was doing the same in his office.

The computer screen lit part of the room while the rest of the lights were off. He knew the time, but only because his mind constantly kept up with every detail around him.

Christian hadn't moved from his computer since Tommy asked him to dinner. He was on to something, and no one else in the country saw it.

Another woman had gone missing on Wednesday. No law enforcement organizations had made the connection because the pattern was almost impossible to see. Christian himself hadn't truly believed it until Wednesday, but now it was staring at him like a bright red line on a map that contained nothing else but black streets.

Five women over two years. One every four months and four months to the day. One from Georgia, where Christian lived. Another in Florida. Then, South Carolina, North Carolina, Virginia, and finally Washington, DC this past Wednesday.

Six missing women over two years wasn't much to go off, and Christian knew it. If he had allowed himself any kind of life outside of work, he would have missed the pattern. Perhaps no one would have seen it. The killer worked at a slow pace and with what appeared to be random abductions.

They're not random, though, Christian thought as he read

over the DC police report again. He didn't need to. His mind had stored all of the information inside his mansion. He re-read it because he wasn't ready to go inside the mansion yet.

Even if he hadn't told Melissa, he knew he was spending too much time there. He found it more comfortable than the actual world. He spent hours each day inside his mansion when before, it had always been a support for life, not life support.

The kidnappings weren't random because of *how* they occurred. Four months, six states, six women, and each one of them had been taken at a bar. Additionally, each woman had been spotted with a man right before the kidnapping. The same description was given for the man each time: dark hair, dark eyes, approximately six feet tall, and white.

Only one bar had a video recording, and Christian had requested a copy last night. He probably wouldn't get it until Wednesday of next week, but if Christian was right, he had four months to catch this guy before another woman went missing.

CHAPTER THREE

"Hey."

Keely Wright's eyes slowly opened.

"Hey," the voice whispered again.

Keely blinked a few times, unsure why she couldn't see anything. Everything before her was black. She couldn't even see the woman who was speaking.

"Can you hear me?" the woman asked. "I don't think he's here anymore. He's at work, wherever the fuck that is."

He? Who is he? Keely wondered, but only for a second. Her mind shoved the confusion away, bringing forth memories that Keely wished with all her heart she didn't have.

Everything came back at once in a cold tidal wave that threatened to drown her. She remembered why it was so dark in here and why she had been asleep to begin with.

The man, *Ted*, had hit her on the head last night.

Why did he hit me? she wondered.

"*Shut Up!*" he had screamed at her. He'd been sitting

right in front of her, legs crossed, and trying to talk to her *as if she wasn't chained to a fucking wall.*

"My name is Sarah," the woman said, and Keely was able to place the woman somewhere on her right. "How's your head? I heard him hit you last night."

"Wh…-Where am I?" Keely asked.

"I don't know. Somewhere in Virginia?"

"I'm not from Virginia," Keely whispered. She slowly sat up against the wall. The chains attached to her hands and feet scraped across the floor, creating an eerie scratching noise.

"Where are you from?"

"DC."

A few seconds of silence passed, then a completely obvious question burst into Keely's mind like a dirty bomb —biological poison floating across her brain.

"He took you too?"

"Yes. But I'm from southern Virginia. So we may not be in either state."

The woman spoke quickly, and Keely didn't know if she understood the importance of her question. She had answered it too fast to *see* what was happening.

"We've been kidnapped," Keely said. "He's kidnapped us. *Kidnapped us!*" Her voice grew shriller with each word, a red panic rising in her mind and blocking out all hope of concentrating on anything else.

"*Hey!*" Sarah yelled, her voice echoing off the walls. "Don't. Freak. Out."

Keely stopped screeching. She heard another voice from across the room. A tiny little scream let loose from someone's mouth. It died as quickly as it was born.

"Who's there?" Keely almost shouted.

"There are other women in here with us," Sarah said. "They don't talk, though. None of them do. I'm the only one who will talk to you, and I think you should listen to me for a little while. Ted will be back soon, and when he is, you're going to want to avoid any more hits to the head."

Keely was quiet. This was too much to take in at once.

"Are you listening to me?" Sarah whispered.

"Yes."

"You can't panic, okay? If you do, you're going to lose it, and when he gets back, he'll hurt you again. The reason these women don't talk is because he's hurt them *a lot*. What's your name?"

Keely didn't notice that no words had come out. Shock was threatening to take over, commanding everything to shut down so it could take her to a place where *this* didn't exist.

"What's your name?" Sarah asked again.

"Keely," she managed to say.

"Okay, Keely. I'm Sarah. I'll tell you what I know, but you have to promise to try and stay calm. Don't freak out on me, okay?"

"Okay," Keely said, though she didn't know how that would be possible.

Ted stood at his basement door without opening it. Last night hadn't gone as he'd wanted. Actually, the past few days hadn't gone as he wanted. Ted was beginning to think it was the women's ages that were creating such discord in his home. The first four had been thirty-five to forty years old. The last two were under thirty. Sarah was *finally* starting to come around, but the past few days with Keely had reminded him so much of Sarah's last four months that he had almost killed her last night.

His knuckles were bruised, and Georgia had noticed them at work. It was the first time she'd noticed something, but that was one time too many.

These goddamn bitches were causing him more trouble than they were worth. It took fucking months to break them in so he could bring them up to the house's ground level and consummate their marriage. *Months.*

If Keely didn't fix her attitude right away, Ted was going to call it quits with her. Maybe Sarah, too, just for the hell she'd already put him through.

"Calm down," Ted whispered.

His hands were clenched in fists and he had to consciously open them, each finger feeling like a massive weight.

It was his weekend to have his daughter, Callie. He didn't want to be dealing with Keely while hanging out with Callie during his visitation time.

Is it getting to be too much? he wondered. *Should you just end it? Maybe you only need a small family. One or two wives. Not six.*

A frown crossed Ted's face at the thought. He wanted a big family. He'd always wanted a big family and didn't see any reason why he shouldn't have one. It had been Christy who only wanted one child. She was the one who had dashed his hopes of a large family.

Ted shook his head, forcing himself to come back to the

moment. He needed to go to the basement and talk with Keely. He needed her to understand that what she'd been doing wouldn't continue any longer.

Ted opened the basement door and walked down the stairs. He always left the door open, although he knew it probably wasn't the smartest thing to do. The basement was pretty much soundproof, but with the door open a neighbor might hear the women if they got loud.

He couldn't bring himself to close the door. He knew how large his shadow looked with the light on behind him. He must look like a god to the women below while descending the stairs.

Ted didn't go directly to Keely. She said nothing as he crossed the basement. He could see the nasty bruise across the side of her face where he'd hit her the previous night. He wasn't going to risk his knuckles anymore. Not for some bitch that hadn't even given him a chance to prove himself.

He went to the toolbox that sat against the wall. He squatted and opened it, rooting around inside until he felt what he was looking for—the rubber mallet. With that in his hand, he walked over to Keely and sat cross-legged in front of her.

"How's your head?" he asked.

Her hands and arms were attached to a chain made up of half-inch links. It was one chain, with four cuffs attached, strung through a clip that he'd bolted into the wall above her. The chain had enough give to allow her to stand but not enough to reach where he was sitting.

Keely said nothing. She stared down at her knees, which she was holding against her chest.

"Keely, I asked you a question," he said.

The girl shook her head slightly, but Ted couldn't tell if she was answering him.

"How. Is. Your. Head?"

Ted's left hand turned into a fist, and his right one curled tighter around the mallet. She had to see the fucking thing, sitting right there in between his legs. She'd seen him go to the toolbox and get it out especially for her. In case she decided to give him more trouble.

But she still wasn't respecting him. Her silence was worse than being screamed at. He wasn't even worth answering, was that what she was trying to say?

"Keely…" He was breathing heavier now, and thoughts of Christy came to his mind. The way she used to make him mad like this, getting under his skin until he could barely talk.

"*Shut the fuck up!*" the woman screamed. She sprang up, her chains losing their slack and straining against the bolt above as she lunged at him. She hung suspended from the chains, leaning forward, her teeth bared at him. "*Let me out! Let me out! Let me the fuck out of here!*"

Ted's left hand uncurled from its fist. He stared at the woman he had risked so much for, transporting her across multiple state lines and bringing her here to his home. To *her* home.

Ted stood, avoiding the woman still leaning forward on the chains. He heard the metal grinding as it supported her weight.

"*Let me out of here!*" she screamed again, her spittle misting Ted's face.

Ted brought the mallet up and slammed it into her temple with a meaty *whack*.

Her head moved in slow motion as it jerked to the right. All her muscles gave out at once, and her right eye bulged forward in her skull as she collapsed to the floor.

Ted stood above her. Her chest moved up and down, although very shallowly. He didn't give much thought to his next decision. He brought the mallet down with two hard smacks, each one landing on the back of her head.

Keely's chest stopped moving.

Ted looked at Sarah. She was standing but hadn't said a word. Her eyes darted to the floor when she saw him looking.

"I…" Ted realized he didn't know what came next.

He dropped the mallet and walked over to Brittany. He wasn't dealing with Sarah today. Or Keely, anymore. He reached into his pocket and pulled out his keys, then reached down and took the cuffs off Brittany. She was docile as he walked her across the basement and up the stairs.

That was why he loved her.

She knew how to act.

He would make love to her, then deal with the mess Keely had created.

———

"You're a son-of-a-bitch," Christy Mackenrow said.

"It can't be helped," her son-of-a-bitch ex-husband, Ted, said.

"Just like it couldn't be helped last time? To be honest, I

don't even care that you don't see her. I prefer it, actually. What I can't stand is having to tell her that you won't be picking her up *again*."

"Tell her I'll see her in two weeks," Ted said.

Christy looked across her kitchen. The old rage had risen again, as it did so easily whenever she spoke to this man. She didn't understand how she'd ever loved him or why she had said yes to his marriage proposal. Except for Callie and the joy she brought, it was the singular worst decision of Christy's life. If she lived a hundred more lifetimes, she wouldn't be able to rival it.

"Fine," she said.

"Thanks."

Christy hung up the phone without saying anything else. She sat stewing in her anger for a few minutes before deciding to get on the exercise bike downstairs. She didn't even bother changing out of her jeans.

She turned on the television, but only to have background noise. She could never focus on anything when Ted got to her like this.

He doesn't sound well, she thought. Then, *Fuck him.*

Callie was only eleven, but it was getting harder and harder to explain Ted's absences. It wasn't like he was a deadbeat. The man was a tenured professor of business, and at a decent school, too. There wasn't any excuse for him blowing his daughter off like this all the time.

How many times has he bothered to see her this year?

She didn't need to count. She knew the number by heart. Six times. He was supposed to have visitation every other weekend, but sometimes he went as long as a month without seeing his daughter. It might be better if he spoke to Callie, but he didn't. He always left Christy to deal with the details.

Maybe she should go back to court and try getting his visitation taken away. She hadn't done it yet because she truly wanted Callie to have her father in her life, but what was *this* doing to her? Would it be better to cut him off so that Callie didn't have to deal with this disappointment?

Sweat popped out across Christy's forehead. She kept pedaling.

She should have never married that man.

While Christy Mackenrow pedaled her exercise bike, Sarah Yields stared at what she thought was a dead body. She hadn't spoken since Ted left the basement, only looked across the basement at Keely.

Ted had left the door open while he was down here, and the light from above shining down had given Sarah a front row ticket to…

Murder. That's what you saw, Sarah-girl. Murder, plain and simple. How'd you like it?

She couldn't believe it, even though Keely wasn't moving.

"Keely," Sarah whispered. When nothing came back, she tried again, her voice harsher. *"Keely!"*

But the body chained to the wall gave no response. Not a single breath exited her lips.

What about the blood you see there in the pale, yellow light, Sarah-girl? Do you think it's a clue that your newfound friend is dead?

The blood looked black against the concrete.

It should be red, shouldn't it? she wondered. A crazy, crazy thought that brought a small giggle to her mouth.

No giggling, Sarah-girl. No more giggling at all. From now on you're going to be quiet in front of Ted because you see what happens if someone isn't. They get the old mallet to the head trick.

Sarah collapsed to the floor, her ass striking first and sending a shudder up her back. Sarah felt none of it. She sat against the wall and stared at the dead girl she had just met days before.

CHAPTER FOUR

Christian stood in front of Tommy and Luke at the conference room whiteboard. He had taped up a large map of the United States and marked six Xs along the East Coast.

"This is serial," he said. "Six women in two years. Each one went missing *exactly* four months after the previous one. They were all last seen in a bar, drinking with a middle-aged man. He's good-looking from most reports. Amicable, too."

"Did someone present this to you?" Tommy asked.

"No. I found it this weekend."

"You found it?"

Christian nodded.

His face looked narrower. Tommy knew that was because he'd lost weight. Christian had always been skinny. Despite eating like a pregnant woman, he never gained a pound. This year, he'd lost weight. He was venturing into haggard territory.

"You want to open an investigation?" Luke asked.

"I think we have to."

Tommy looked at Luke, who was leaning back in his chair. These two guys were much smarter than he'd ever be, and Tommy had no problem admitting it. He wanted to know what Luke thought about Christian's newest theory.

"Do we have any recordings from the bars?"

"One bar had video. A copy is being shipped. It should be here today."

"They don't have a digital copy?"

Christian shrugged. "It was a dive bar in Florida. We're lucky they have anything at all."

"What did the report say about the tape? Does it show the suspect?" Tommy asked.

"Yes. You can see him talking to her at the bar from what I gathered."

"Did they put out his picture to the press?"

"Local, yes, but national, no," Christian said.

"You willing to go to Waverly with this?" Tommy asked.

If Christian wanted to tell FBI Director Alan Waverly that he thought they had a serial killer on their hands, then so be it. Tommy didn't feel strongly about this one way or another. The three of them had a full caseload as it was, and he wouldn't be going back to all-night shifts just because Christian thought he saw something in the shadows.

"Once I get a look at the tape, yeah," Christian said.

"What do you think, Luke?"

"Fidelity, bravery, integrity," Luke said with a little smile, repeating the FBI slogan.

"Thanks. Mind not fucking around?"

"Let's look at the tape," Luke said. "We'll decide after

that."

"The recording's here," Christian said into his office phone. "Bring Luke down, too."

"Okay," Tommy said. "Be right there."

Christian hung up the phone and pulled out the disk from the large white envelope. He'd half-expected the backwoods police department to send him an actual tape, but it appeared they did have some technology down there even if they hadn't been able to email him a copy.

He stuck the CD into his computer and opened the video application.

Luke and Tommy entered a minute later.

"Let's see what ya got," Tommy said as they moved behind his computer.

Christian hit play, and they watched the video.

Ten minutes passed with no one saying a word. There was no audio to the recording. They let it roll in silence, watching the man and woman talk to each other.

It ended when the man and woman walked out of the camera's view.

"The person I emailed with said the cut only showed the part where the couple was visible," Christian said, turning his chair around to look at his two partners.

"They only spoke for ten minutes?" Tommy said.

"That's all they got on camera. I looked at the bar's blueprint. It's fairly large, but there are only two cameras. One pointed at the bar, and one in the back office pointed at the safe."

"The only two places they keep money," Luke said.

"Yup."

"Well, that's not a lot to go off, Christian. What else is in the police report? What did witnesses say? Interviews with family?" Tommy asked.

"The woman's name was Brittany Seabrook. She's thirty-nine and was out with her friends, no special event. She's recently divorced. Her ex-husband was out of town and had an alibi that checked out. Friends said they saw her leave with the man on the tape and that Brittany called them an hour later when she got to the man's hotel room—"

"Hotel room?" Luke interrupted.

"Yeah. He was there 'on business.' On a Saturday night. Brittany might have noticed the discrepancy if she hadn't been three hours deep into drinking. When her friends called her the next morning, no answer. By that afternoon her phone was off."

"Did the police check cell tower records? GPS locations?"

"Yeah, it appears they did some detective work on this one. The phone was found in a trashcan behind a restaurant. The waitstaff said the couple came in at about two in the morning, ate, paid cash, and left. That was the last time either were seen."

"Let me guess. The restaurant had no recording system, did it?" Tommy asked.

"Nope."

"I doubt there was a hotel room," Luke said.

"That's gutsy," Tommy said. "Showing up at a bar and hoping to get someone intoxicated enough to take home, then kidnapping them?"

"No gutsier than any other kidnapping," Christian said. "Men go out every weekend hoping for the exact same thing, sans the kidnapping, and add an orgasm to it. The only difference here is this man put her in the trunk of a car instead of a bed."

Tommy didn't think Christian knew much about what regular guys did on weekends. As far as he knew, the kid had never once gone out hoping to find a woman for sex. He'd lost his virginity to Veronica.

None of *that* mattered. Tommy was working out his thoughts. Christian didn't need to hear any of it. He had already decided that these missing women were related, and nothing his partners said would change his mind.

"What do you want to do?" Tommy turned to Christian and crossed his arms.

"Tell Waverly. Then go to DC and investigate the last kidnapping."

"What about our current caseload?" Luke asked.

"They're active, but they're not *active* like this is. In four more months, there'll be another kidnapping on the coast that follows this exact pattern. I guarantee it."

"All right," Tommy said. "Let's see if we can get on Waverly's calendar tomorrow."

"Why not try to call him now?" Christian said.

"One, because he's the director and this isn't an active case. It's a pitch. Two, it's four o'clock and I've got to wrap up some emails to get out of here by five."

An arrow of disgust shot through Christian's mind. "What happened to you? Are you tired of working hard?"

The two people in front of him were quiet for a second

before Tommy said, "No, I just realized that life is pretty good, and I can't experience it in this building. Thanks for your concern, Christian."

He walked out of the room without saying anything else. Christian turned his chair and watched him go, part of him wanting to apologize, but another part said, *Let him go. He'll get over it.*

Luke walked around to the front of Christian's desk and stood waiting for Tommy to walk down the hall. Once he was out of sight, Luke turned to Christian. "Nice of you to say."

"Two years ago he would have been here working with me all night," Christian said. "It's not my fault he's lost his drive."

"How many nights have you slept here in a row?"

Christian was startled by the question. He had been careful about sleeping here, ensuring that he had a fresh change of clothes each time and keeping a small bag of toiletries in his messenger bag to make sure he appeared fresh.

He'd been foolish to think he could hide it from Luke.

"Today's Wednesday, so I'm guessing since Monday," his partner said.

Christian nodded.

"Why aren't you going home?"

"I'm trying to catch killers."

"The killers sleep. You should, too."

Christian was quiet for a few seconds, staring at Luke with unforgiving eyes. "You know why I'm here. You better than anyone."

"I asked you to step into the winter, Christian. I never asked you to make it your home."

The winter. Christian hadn't thought of his life like that before, but Luke always portrayed things in new ways. *Correct* ways.

He didn't know how to respond, so he said the only thing that came to his mind. "How's Veronica?"

"She misses you. I tell her it's not in her best interest to contact you. How's the winter?"

"Better than summer," Christian said. "See you tomorrow, Luke."

"Have a good night," his partner answered and walked out of the office.

Christian swiveled his chair around and looked out the window. He'd pissed off both of them in less than five minutes. Tommy was hurt. No one could hurt Luke. He probably wasn't even upset.

That had been Luke without any of society's conventions hanging around his neck.

Does a baby ask to be born? Christian thought. *No, they're brought into this world without a choice.*

You had a choice.

That voice was his own, but it belonged to the Other and only existed in Christian's head. If he turned his chair around, he'd see the replica of himself standing at the door.

Christian had seen visions like this ever since he was a little boy. At first they had only been of his mother, then Melissa once his psychiatrist came into the fold. Those two helped him deal with the world when it became overwhelming, when he needed to calm down.

This person, this Other... Christian wasn't sure why he

came. Or, if he knew the reason, he didn't want to admit it even to himself.

You had a choice and made it, and every day since then, you've been making the same choice. Because you like it. Why haven't you been to the mansion lately? There's a lot waiting there for you, especially about this new case, the Other said.

Christian knew the Other wasn't lying. He'd spent almost a solid week thinking about these kidnappings, with only a few hours of sleep interrupting when it was absolutely necessary. His mind had created a whole room, and it was ready for him, filled with insights that could have helped when introducing this theory to Luke and Tommy.

He hadn't gone, and now the Other was asking him why.

"I don't want to," he said.

Not this again. We went through all that months ago, but you stepped into the winter, as Luke called it. It is better than summer, Christian. You know that.

No one else was in the room. If they had been, they would have heard a one-sided conversation and quite possibly thought Christian insane. He didn't usually speak to the mental images projected onto reality. His mother had always told him it was fine to do so, but he didn't want to scare people so it was best just to let the images do the talking.

Christian didn't care about scaring people anymore.

"Are you going to leave me alone to work if I go inside?" Christian asked.

Of course. Mi casa, su casa.

CHAPTER FIVE

Veronica Lopez was tired as she stepped from her car. It was new, but as she parked it behind Luke's, she felt as she always did. Luke had style that was hard to match.

She was here for her psychiatry appointment. She'd been seeing Luke since Bradley Brown had decided to strap her down to a bed and attempt playing surgeon on a bunch of people.

Veronica was tired, but she never missed her sessions with Luke unless she was too sick to get out of bed, which had only happened once since she started therapy.

Luke helped tremendously, and she knew how special his time was. Even after so many years, she still understood that an hour with her wasn't worth his time, not in the larger scheme of things. His mind was capable of feats that could change the world, and agreeing to spend it changing her life was a gesture that money couldn't ever repay.

Veronica heard the door open and pulled her eyes from his new car.

"You look tired," Luke called.

She smiled and walked to him. "I'm not sleeping well."

"Are you taking the pills I prescribed?"

She shook her head.

"Come in and tell me why," he said.

He let her walk in, then closed the door behind them. They made their way to Luke's living room and sat in their usual spots, him on a chair and her on a couch with a single glass table separating them.

Veronica never saw him move his living room around, but she knew he did to accommodate her sessions. She appreciated it and understood why he did it. She became the center of the room and his attention.

"I don't want to be drugged to cope anymore," Veronica said. "I've been on antidepressants since Brown and sleeping pills since that bitch Speckle. I really want to come off it all."

"Why?" Luke asked.

"I never needed medication before. I don't want to need it for the rest of my life."

"Do you remember why I prescribed the antide-pressants?"

Veronica nodded, remembering it well. She had been a wreck after Brown kidnapped her. Crying uncontrollably. Depressed. Wild mood swings. Night terrors. The whole gambit of post-traumatic stress symptoms.

"If I take you off the antidepressants, you may experi-ence depression again. I want you to be aware of the possibility."

"I know." She sighed. "I know. I just… I don't want to be dependent on medication to keep living."

Luke smiled. "At least you don't have to worry about addiction, then."

"Not to drugs." She didn't finish the sentence with what she wanted to say: *Only to Christian.*

"If you want to come off the antidepressants, we'll need to taper it gradually. SSRIs can have side effects if you quit too quickly."

Veronica nodded, wanting to change the subject. She didn't like going against Luke's advice. She trusted him too much. If he said she needed to stay on them, then she would for now.

"I had a dream last night. I've had it every night this past week."

"The same one?"

"Yes."

"Have you had it before this past week?"

Veronica shook her head. "I'm standing outside of this huge building. It's massive, stretching into the clouds and running miles in both directions. I want to get inside, but none of the doors are open. The windows are all on the second story and I can't get up there. I feel like I walked forever last night, trying to find an open door."

"Do you think the building is Christian?"

"I was hoping it wouldn't be something so obvious," she said.

"Christian isn't well, Veronica."

It was the first time Luke had said something about how Christian was doing since their breakup. He never spoke about Christian's wellbeing, only Veronica's and what would be in *her* best interest. "What do you mean?"

"The change you've seen in him isn't about you at all. I

thought that he was trying to protect you and that's why he refused to continue your relationship. I was wrong. He needs help, I think."

Veronica stared at Luke. His angular, thin face showed calm even though his voice was laden with concern.

"Why are you telling me this?"

"Do you not want to know?"

"You know I do, but I can't help him. He won't take my calls. Last time I showed up at his house, he wouldn't answer the door, and I'm not about to commit breaking and entering."

Luke nodded but said nothing.

"Do you think I should contact him?"

Luke crossed one leg over the other. "I think someone has to reach him, Veronica. I'm scared of what he might do."

CHAPTER SIX

Waverly got the team onto his calendar quickly. On Monday morning, Tommy had asked the director's assistant about availability, and Waverly had them on a plane that evening for a meeting the next morning.

The flight was short and uneventful. Luke spent it with his eyes closed, hoping that Tommy wouldn't talk to him. Christian sat in the middle, but Luke knew he wouldn't speak unless spoken to.

Luke wondered if Veronica had reached out to Christian yet. Luke hadn't directly suggested that *she* should, only left it in the air that something was desperately wrong with her poor, lost lover. That would be enough. Luke knew she would try speaking with him as soon as she built up the nerve.

He was in a holding pattern right now, arranging things without being completely sure what would happen with Veronica chasing Christian again. He couldn't be confident his plans would go exactly as he wanted. More, he wasn't sure exactly what he wanted out of the impending contact.

The end result would be Luke attaining his desire. Veronica would die. Horribly.

Luke hadn't forgotten about her offense all those years ago when she'd tried to recruit Christian to help in her investigation of Luke's possible murders. While John Presley had caused his own death, Veronica was responsible for it, too.

Going to him and asking those questions had sealed Mr. Presley's fate and his wife's.

That Luke was guilty of the things Veronica had thought had no bearing on the situation.

She had gone back into his academic past, discovering that Luke's boss had committed suicide after having a public tiff with Luke over his involvement in the Sphere.

Luke had killed Trevor Rollins for that tiff.

His eyes still closed, Luke thought back to the day in Dr. Rollins' house. The man had been terrified. His button-down Oxford shirt was soaked through with sweat.

He had bound the man to the chair using zip-ties. Luke hadn't covered the man's mouth. He wanted Dr. Rollins to be able to speak.

"What the fuck are you doing, Luke?" the man had demanded when he woke up strapped to his kitchen chair.

"I'm making sure that you don't cause me any more trouble."

That was when Rollins had understood Luke's plan and quite possibly *thought* he saw Luke's insanity. Luke wasn't insane. No, he was probably a bit *too* rational, if truth be told.

"Whatever you're thinking about doing, don't." Dr. Rollins had been trying to remain calm, hoping he could talk himself out of this like he had seen in so many movies.

However, fear couldn't be hidden by someone that didn't practice. His voice had carried a live undercurrent of electricity, and his eyes darted every which way in the vain hope of finding something that might help him.

Luke had picked up the shotgun from the couch and showed it to Dr. Rollins. "I haven't had a long career, but up until you, my reputation was spotless."

The man had let out a cry that sounded like a shrill bird calling a mate at the sight of the weapon.

"I can't abide someone tainting my reputation, Trevor. Dr. Trevor Rollins." Luke had rolled the full name off his tongue, tasting it like wine. "You see, we only have two things in this world. Reputation and purpose. Reputation allows one to complete their purpose, and if mine is destroyed, my purpose will be hampered. I can't allow that to happen."

"I'll resign tomorrow," the man had vowed. "I'll leave the state. I'll leave the goddamn *country*. Just don't do whatever you're wanting to do with that!" His words had picked up speed as he spoke, fear tightening its grip on him.

"It's too late for that, Trevor. You remember when we spoke in your office *two months ago?*"

Dr. Rollins nodded. Neither of them said anything else for a second. Luke gave him time to take in the consequences of those words.

Dr. Rollins had summoned Luke to his office and told him that he was to quit either his private psychiatry practice or his work on the Sphere. His teaching was suffering, and that wouldn't be tolerated.

"You didn't listen to me when I said that I don't do well with ultimatums, Trevor. You thought I was bluffing. Now you see I wasn't."

Luke had taken the man's right shoe off. Dr. Rollins began blubbering and begging. Luke had ignored him and worked slowly, taking the sock off next and setting both neatly to the side.

"Open your mouth, please," Luke had said.

Dr. Rollins opened it, but only to release a string of pleas. Luke shoved the shotgun barrel in deep, careful not to damage the man's teeth. He then bent back down to Dr. Rollins's right foot and hooked his toe over the trigger. The man had gone deathly still, not wanting to accidentally set the gun off. Even at the end, hoping to be saved.

Luke had looked up at him and said, "When you see God, tell him I said hello."

A small smile crossed Luke's face as he remembered slamming the man's foot down on the trigger and the resulting explosion of Dr. Rollins' head.

It had been a glorious red.

"No tie today, Windsor?" Director Alan Waverly asked.

Tommy had noticed Christian's lack of a tie and said something earlier. Christian had ignored him. One didn't show up to the director's office dressed in business casual. No one besides Christian, apparently.

"I didn't want to worry about the knot," he said.

Waverly smiled, and Tommy knew why. Waverly had

told him that when Christian first met the director, he'd been terrified his knot wasn't right.

Tommy knew that Christian had left the tie in the hotel room for a different reason. He didn't know exactly why, only that it had nothing to do with worrying about a knot. Maybe it was his autism, but maybe not.

"I read the preliminaries, and I'm willing to bite on the case if your plan sounds good. I want to stress that I don't want this turning into a media circus. Right now, no one else knows about this, right?"

"That's right," Christian said, taking the lead without being asked. "None of the states have been in contact with each other. Local media reported on the incidents when they occurred, but since then there have been no follow-ups."

"What about the families? Has anyone made a stink out of the lack of progress?"

"No," Christian said.

Waverly nodded and looked down at the dossier Christian had created. All four had one in front of them. Tommy had read his last night, the first time in a while he'd worked after the sun went down. He hadn't had anything else to do in the hotel room, although he was careful to make sure he was asleep by midnight.

"Okay, tell me your plan," Waverly said.

"I'd... *We'd* like to begin with the woman who went missing last week in DC. It's the latest kidnapping and will have the most active leads."

"I take it your current caseload won't get in the way?"

Christian needed to walk carefully here, but Tommy couldn't tell him that. The director was *always* attuned to media attention, knowing that if the FBI was caught ignoring cases for something that might not even exist, a firestorm could ensue.

"No, sir. The three of us decided we can work our current load with this addition."

No such conversation had taken place, although Tommy wouldn't say that right now.

"Fair enough. So you'll start investigating here. Your report says someone else will turn up missing in four months. If no one does, are you going to call this off?"

Christian nodded. "Yes, sir."

"I suppose I didn't need to call you three up here for a meeting, but I wanted to see how serious you were. You've never brought anything to me before. I wanted to make sure you really thought something was here. You do?"

"Have I been wrong yet?" Christian asked, meeting the director's eyes.

Tommy was taken aback by the question. Christian always said inappropriate things in front of people, including Waverly, but *this* was different. Inappropriate, but not driven by his normal fear.

The director looked at him evenly for a few seconds. "No, I suppose you haven't." He smiled. "Go forth, then, and catch the kidnapper." He turned to Tommy. "Do you have a few minutes to meet with me?"

"Yes, sir," Tommy said, surprised for the second time in moments. He waited while his two partners shook the director's hand and exited his office.

Standing, Waverly walked over to his window, leaving Tommy sitting at the conference table.

"What's wrong with him?"

Tommy didn't need to ask who he was talking about. Christian was making waves now, and Tommy hoped to hell *he* knew it. If the director was noticing the changes, that was a problem.

"Sir," Tommy started.

"Listen, this is off the record. We go back before I was director, and I'm asking you as a colleague."

Tommy nodded and did turn around then. "What happened with Speckle has gotten to him, I think."

"I'm sure Luke's noticed it, too."

"Yes, sir."

"Have you had anyone from the FBI look at him? One of our psychologists?"

"No, sir," Tommy said.

"What do you think is wrong with him?"

"Sir, I'm not a psychologist. I wouldn't venture to say."

"Jesus, Tommy, just tell me what I'm asking." The director turned from the window and met Tommy's gaze.

"I think he's scared to death of getting people hurt. I think he's cutting off everyone in his life so that this job can't affect them."

"It's more than that. The tie thing. Then the question he asked me about having never been wrong." The director shook his head and looked down. "He's different. I'm going to have a psychologist talk to him, and if he asks you anything, you tell him to call me, okay?"

Tommy swallowed. "Yes, sir."

"I'll have someone reach out today. I know you think that will be too obvious, but I want it to be. He needs to know that whatever is going on is being noticed. I also don't want him snapping in the field. We've got to bring him back onto the range. Do you understand what I'm saying?"

"I do, sir."

"What did he say to you?" Christian asked.

Luke sat with Tommy and Christian in the hotel room. It was five in the morning, and they'd already had a full day of work ahead, but now Waverly had thrown a wrench in their plans.

"What do you think he said, Christian?" Tommy was in the bathroom, straightening his tie in the mirror.

Luke saw that Christian had decided to wear one, deciding that the knot wouldn't be a bother today. Luke liked the rebellion the boy had shown yesterday.

"I'm asking *you*," Christian said. He was pacing in front of the bed, looking down at his feet.

"You went in there without a fucking tie on. You asked him a question about whether or not you had ever been wrong. You showed nothing but arrogance, and so he asked me what was wrong with you."

"What did you tell him?"

Christian's rage was bubbling under the surface, and Luke loved it. He hadn't seen this part of Christian, but he had hoped it might arise. Rage was good. It was something that could be harnessed and set in motion on a specific target.

Tommy came to stand in the bathroom doorway. When he spoke, his voice was calm, and Luke knew he didn't like what he heard in Christian's voice.

"I told him that what happened with Speckle changed you. I told him I thought you were doing everything you could to keep people you care about safe, and that the easiest way to do that was to keep them at bay. If you're upset, I'm sorry, Christian, but when the director asks me a question, I answer it. I answered truthfully because I care about you and I'm worried. Luke is, too."

Christian stopped walking and looked at Luke in his chair. "That true? You're worried about me?"

"I've noticed the changes, yes. It's concerning."

"That's thoughtful of you, Tommy. I appreciate your candor with the director. I just hope that these new therapy sessions don't interrupt my work so much that someone else ends up dead since I know you won't make up for the time I'll be missing."

Christian walked out of the room, slamming the door behind him.

"Jesus," Tommy said.

"He's perturbed."

"Just a bit."

Luke smiled as Tommy stepped out of the bathroom and grabbed his jacket.

"Ready to go?" Luke asked.

"Yeah."

Luke followed him out of the hotel room, happy with the morning's turn of events. Waverly had always been a pest. Luke had wondered for a while if he should kill the director, but now it seemed he might help Luke's plans.

A new psychologist in the mix was a good thing. The more people swimming around in Christian's head, the better.

Christian sat on the couch and looked across the room at Dr. Michael Hanson. The man was older than him. Christian tagged him at around forty-nine. He hadn't time to look up anything about the man since Waverly had sent him a personal email at four in the morning, saying he needed to be at Hanson's office by seven.

"What do you know about me?" Christian asked, the first thing either of them had said since he'd arrived.

"I read what I could last night. This case was given to me on short notice, as I'm sure it was for you."

"What did you read?"

"You're having a remarkable career so far. You've had some tough run-ins on very high-profile crimes."

"Anything else?" Christian wanted to push the man as far as possible, as quickly as possible.

"You are a high-functioning autistic. You show symptoms of Asperger's. Your IQ is in the upper echelon of the population."

The man wasn't shaken by the questions. Christian's mind was drawing conclusions based on the few sentences exchanged. This man had seen a lot in his years with the FBI. He'd dealt with criminals and agents, and Christian's rage wouldn't divert him from whatever goal Waverly had laid out.

"Why am I here?" Christian felt exhaustion along with his anger leaving; a black-winged creature perched on his back flying away.

"Well, the most direct reason would be that Waverly is

concerned about you. I will say I've never had him email me directly about a patient. You're the first."

"Okay. What can you tell Waverly about our conversations in here?"

"Your contract with the FBI does somewhat interfere with doctor-patient confidentiality. I'm legally allowed to give him summaries about your mental state, as well as my reasoning behind those summaries."

"Will he see detailed conversations?"

"I can give him those if I want. I most likely won't. I do prefer there be some sense of privacy."

Christian nodded and looked down at his feet. "All right. We have forty-five minutes. Where do you want to start?"

"If you don't mind, I'm curious about what goes on inside your head. The director didn't mention it, but the crimes you've solved are well known. The leaps you make in cases are looked at with awe. Would you mind starting there?"

"Not at all," Christian said, a sad smile spreading across his face. "Let's look at the caged monkey and see what goes on when he doesn't think anyone's watching."

FOR CHRISTIAN WINDSOR

Christian,

We began our investigation on the case you discovered. Well done on the early detective work. I believe you're right. These women are being abducted by the same person. Of course, you won't see this letter until that person's fate has already been decided, but I still want you to know I admire your abilities.

What's happening to you right now is fairly simple, even if you're unable to see it.

You crossed a barrier with Lucy Speckle, and I helped push you through it. Blame can't be laid solely at my feet. Sooner or later, you would have walked to that barrier on your own. You, out of everyone on Earth, cannot live next to winter and not begin feeling its biting cold. I'm not sure if you would have entered the season without my assistance, but your choice of career would have brought you right up to it, regardless.

You're becoming like the people you're chasing, Christian.

Not deranged as they all are, of course. Your change is modeling by their disregard for social norms. Their desires rise above the demands of their community, and so when they reach out to scoop someone's eyes from a skull, they don't see it as wrong. To them, their desires must be fed above all else.

I found a quote by a man named Albert Fish. He was a very, very deranged individual, but I find what he said to be applicable to you.

"I am a man of passion. You don't know what that means unless you are my kind. At the orphanage they put me just before Garfield was assassinated, there were some older boys that caught a horse in a sloping field. They got the horse up against a fence down at the bottom of the field and tied him up. An old horse. They put kerosene on his tail and lit it and cut the rope. Away went that old horse, bursting through fences to get away from the fire. But the fire went with him. That horse, that's me. That's the man of passion. The fire chases you and catches you and then it's in your blood. And after that, it's the fire that has control and not the man. Blame the fire of passion for what Albert H. Fish has done."

You and Albert are growing more and more similar than you know. Your desires, your passions, *are going to start driving you more and more, Christian.*

I can't wait to see what you're capable of.

Yours,

Luke Titan, MD, Ph.D., Special Agent for the Federal Bureau of Investigations

CHAPTER SEVEN

Ted had canceled on his daughter this weekend because he wasn't about to let a whole four months go before he struck again. He needed another lover to add to his growing family, and he couldn't let the last fuckup stop that.

Christy would have to get over it. She was the caricature of an ex-wife. Always nagging, always bitching, and always trying to take away *his* daughter.

Ted was back in DC. He had gotten another flight on Friday afternoon and taken off from work early. He didn't have any classes after eleven in the morning, so he'd finished his emails and gone right to the airport.

The first woman he'd taken from Georgia had been the easiest, but he found it almost frightening how simple it was to get these women back to his house. He had taken a plane to his destination and a car back, keeping them drugged and in the trunk the whole ride. Ted had never been pulled over, and if he was, so what? He was white, male, and had a Ph.D. No one would bother him.

He was, of course, using different states to keep people from noticing. He thought DC would be okay again. The town was full of crime. He liked the nightlife, too. That was something else Christy never appreciated, going out and having a few drinks. He killed two birds with the proverbial single stone each time he did this. He had a night on the town and helped his family grow larger.

Ted stayed in a nice hotel each time, and this one was no exception.

He looked at himself in the mirror and admired his appearance. "You look great," he said to the bathroom mirror.

For his late-thirties, he was a good-looking man, and the ease with which he spoke to women provided even more evidence of that fact.

Ted finished up and left the hotel room. It would be a good night. He had no idea that by the end of it he would meet Christian Windsor.

Christian hated being away from home, and he was still in DC on Friday evening. Today had been long, and not just because he'd gone to Hanson's for the second time this week.

He supposed he could have flown home for the weekend. Tommy had. Luke and Christian had decided to stay. Christian didn't want to waste time flying when he could be working, but he wasn't sure why Luke had stayed, and it didn't occur to him to ask.

It was about nine at night, and while the city around

him was just getting started for the weekend, Christian was in his hotel room with his eyes closed and the lights off around him.

He was in his mansion.

The name engraved above the room said *The Lover.*

The name put a different hue on things, giving him a different view of the person committing these crimes.

Christian entered the room. The door closed behind him without him touching it. Christian hadn't seen the Other since entering, and he didn't know if he preferred that or not.

He had, at one point, hated the Other being here, but now Christian felt a sense of comfort from his presence.

Mi casa, su casa, the other had said.

Christian chuckled. The Other was arrogant, no doubt about it. Christian had built this place, and it was *his.* It would always be *his.*

Christian looked at the room that existed only in his mind, observing what his subconscious had created. Six women's pictures were placed on the digital walls in front of him, two on each. They were positioned chronologically, the first one taken on the left and the last to Christian's right. Digital police reports were laid out to the side of each woman's picture, available for Christian to peruse if necessary.

He wasn't interested in the reports. They were all memorized.

Another person stood in the room with him, and it wasn't the Other. The person standing in front of him wasn't aware of Christian. He was a projection of Christian's mind.

He looked at the kidnapper, who was standing in front of the last picture to Christian's right. The kidnapper stared at her, noticing nothing else inside the room. Christian could only see his back. He wore the same clothes as the video recording.

"Why are you looking only at her?" Christian wondered.

The man shook his head.

"You do love them," Christian whispered.

The man reached into his pocket and pulled out a marker. Without any hesitation, he took off the lid and drew a large red X across the woman's face.

The screen behind her didn't darken, but Christian knew what it meant. The woman was dead, but the other five were alive.

Why? Why her? he wondered.

The man turned from the red X and placed the marker back in his pocket. He walked by Christian without noticing him, as if he wasn't there. He opened the door behind Christian and left the room.

The door shut, leaving Christian alone again.

"This is weird," he said.

"Things are changing in here," the Other said from the vent.

"I don't like it."

"You will later."

"No, I won't," Christian said. "This isn't supposed to be a place of riddles for me."

"You're never one for fun, Christian," the Other said.

The room went silent, and Christian knew the Other had left.

The room didn't change, despite Christian's protest. The woman to his right, Keely Wright, was dead, and The Lover had killed her.

The door behind Christian swung open.

"Come with me," the Other said. "I want to show you something I've been working on."

Christian turned and followed without saying anything. He walked down the hallway behind his replica. Blood dripped from the Other's hand, leaving a trail of droplets along his path.

"Here," the Other said, stopping at a room Christian hadn't seen before. He looked at the sign above, carved in stone like all the other names.

Us, it read.

"You and I should have a place to speak so I don't interrupt you when you're working. Sound nice?"

Christian looked at the Other's face for the first time since arriving. He was smiling, as always. No blood ran from his mouth, but bloody tears leaked from his eyes, running down his face like horrible rain.

"Go on," the Other said. "It's ready."

Christian opened the door to the new room and went inside. The Other followed behind.

"It's beautiful," Christian said, unable to help himself.

Large, stone Greek statues sat in the room's four corners. Christian didn't know the artists or the statues' names, but he made a note to figure them out.

Two large, overstuffed chairs with high backs sat in the middle of the room. They were clearly antiques. The leather looked worn yet extremely comfortable. A circular glass table with a gray metal stand sat between them. Two glasses of water sat on the table.

"I know you won't drink out of them, but I thought they were a nice touch," the Other said.

Above the table was a single light that sat inside the ceiling.

"Come sit with me," the Other said as he walked to the chair on the left.

"That's what Luke used to say when I'd show up at his house." Christian didn't move.

"Is it?" the Other asked, still crying those bloody tears. Still smiling.

Christian walked to the second chair and sat.

"There are no riddles in here, Christian. The way you see things is changing. Or rather, the way your mind communicates them to you. I need a bigger space in your life, and so our conversations will take the place of what you once saw in those rooms."

"You don't need any more space," Christian said.

"It doesn't matter what you think, and you know it."

Christian was quiet, only looking at the brown eyes in front of him. They were clear, despite the tears that continually leaked down the Other's face.

"He's going to kidnap again," the Other said, "and soon. If I had to guess, I'd say this weekend."

"Why did he kill the woman on the wall?"

"I can't say, although I'm fairly certain it happened. My mind is your mind, Christian, and you know we can't always decipher how it comes up with what it does."

"Something happened to her, though?"

The Other nodded and Christian knew it was true. Keely Wright was no longer alive, but the others were.

"He loves them?" Christian asked.

"Yes. In his own way. He is the Lover, as much as Lucy Speckle was the Priestess."

"Why does he kidnap them if he loves them?"

"His sense of love is warped," the Other said.

Christian didn't like his diction. It sounded far too much like Luke's. Clipped and precise.

"Why are you talking like Luke?"

"You created me, Christian. You tell me."

Christian looked away at the statue in the right corner. He didn't focus on it. He needed to decide whether the Other's speaking pattern or the killer was more important.

"He'll go north next," Christian said, mostly to himself.

"I don't think so."

"Why not?" Christian's eyes moved back to his mirror image.

"He wants someone from every state. We thought he was doing that to keep the police off his trail, and he probably is, but there's more to it. Think about the women. Are they similar?"

"No," Christian said immediately. His mind fed him all the available details. "The first four were a bit older, but all in their thirties. The second two were in their twenties. Two brunettes. Two blondes. A redhead, and the last woman had green hair."

"Exactly. He's taking different types each time because—"

"He's trying out different types of women. He wants to see which one fits him best," Christian finished.

"Yes. He's taking them from multiple states to see what difference it makes in their personas. But he doesn't have anyone from DC, not after poor Keely's demise, and that's a very different place than southern Virginia."

"So he's coming back here."

"And soon," the Other said.

Christian dressed quickly, knowing that he was already running late. He didn't know much about weekend nightlife. Actually, he knew very, very little, but it stood to reason that ten at night meant the weekly ritual of drinking oneself into oblivion had already begun.

He tore through his suitcase quickly, having no idea what the hell to wear. Finally, he settled on the suit he'd worn to see Waverly. Blue slacks and blazer, and a white button-down.

It would have to work.

Christian raced to the elevator and from there out of the building, requesting an Uber as he ran.

He didn't call Luke. He had learned his lesson about involving others.

He had learned it well.

Luke watched Christian rush out of the hotel as if it were ablaze from the parking lot across the street, sitting in the car he'd rented earlier in the afternoon.

Tommy had gone home, planning on returning Sunday

evening. Luke knew he would have pushed that to Monday morning if possible. He was *dedicated* to the work-life balance idea.

Luke had stayed, and when Tommy asked why, he'd said to keep an eye on Christian.

He wasn't lying. Luke couldn't see inside Christian's head, but he knew the boy well enough to venture a guess that Christian would make a leap in the case. Luke had offered dinner with Christian but was turned down, as expected.

Luke preferred eating by himself, anyway. The worst part about dating Riley was that she always wanted to eat with him. Eat and talk. Eat and talk. Humans were an odd species. Other animals ate in silence, only communicating to growl at a member of their group encroaching too closely.

Luke watched Christian enter the Uber, then started his vehicle. He hated the engine's noise. The entire car was uncomfortable, but one must make do with what one had.

He pulled out of the parking lot and followed his partner into the night.

CHAPTER EIGHT

Mary Lawson thought the man in front of her was just too damn cute. Perhaps even gorgeous, although a part of her said maybe the alcohol was thinking *that*.

"What's your name again?" she asked.

The man smiled, his teeth perfect and white even in the club's dark atmosphere. "Ted. Think you'll remember this time?"

"Hush!" she said, lightly slapping his shoulder. She took a sip of her drink, still smiling at him.

"Where did your friends go?" Ted asked.

Mary looked around, squinting as she attempted to look through the crowd of people. "I don't know. They're here somewhere."

"Do you need to go find them?"

Mary laughed. "Are you trying to get rid of me?"

"No way. I'm trying to hold on to you forever."

His smile was *sexy*.

"How old are you?" Mary asked.

"Thirty-eight. You?"

"Twenty-nine."

"Oh my God. I'm way too old for you."

"No! I like older men," Mary said. She couldn't *stop* smiling around this guy. It was like everything he said was exactly the right thing. "Guys my age are just now starting to…I don't know…"

"Become men?"

"Ha! Exactly!" Mary glanced around the club again for her friends, but she didn't see them. She briefly wondered if she should find them. However, she was *also* wondering what it would be like to finish the night with Ted. She hadn't had sex in a while, and he *did* seem like a nice guy.

"Do you live around here?"

"No, I'm here on business," Ted said.

"That sucks! I won't be able to see you again."

"Not true. I come here a lot on business."

"Oh, that's interesting. What do you do?"

As the conversation continued, the night grew later. Mary Lawson found that she wasn't running out of things to talk about with Ted, and she liked that.

A lot.

Christian knew there were thousands of bars in downtown DC, so he only had one option to catch the guy, and it wasn't a good one. Go back to the bar where Keely Wright was last seen.

The chance was small. Infinitesimally so, actually. But maybe the kidnapper would return to the same fishing hole.

Christian entered the club without feeling awkward. Normally, he wouldn't have even looked at a place like this from the street, but right now his mind was in control, not his personality.

He walked to an empty table in the back. The place wasn't packed yet, but it was more than full enough for Christian. No waitress came over, and he figured it was too late for that type of interaction. If you wanted something, you went to the bar.

Christian kept his eyes moving around the room, looking for the man he'd seen on the video. He would stay here all night, waiting until he either found him or the club closed. Most likely, the club would close.

An hour passed and Christian didn't move from the table. It was too dark in this place, and the later it got, the more people piled in, making it harder and harder to see.

He finally stood and started walking around. He'd do laps if necessary.

Luke recognized the awkwardness if he was caught. However, if Christian saw him, an explanation would be easy enough.

He stood at the corner of the bar with a scotch in front of him. The people bustling around him were grating on his composure. The aggressiveness with which they moved and spoke caused Luke no end of annoyance. They were all fools and in his way.

Still, Luke could see Christian from where he stood, yet he remained hidden when Christian came his way. Luke would know immediately if Christian saw him. The boy wouldn't be able to control his reaction.

Christian wasn't on a woman-finding mission. Luke saw that Christian's *mind* controlled him now, thinking faster than perhaps anyone else in the world. He was looking at individuals and dismissing them, which meant he thought the kidnapper was here.

Why? Luke wondered. What occurred this evening to give him that idea? It seemed ridiculous or would have if it wasn't coming from Christian.

No, if Christian figured there was a chance the man might return, Luke trusted him.

For all of Luke's genius, he truly was impressed with Christian's abilities. The boy didn't understand them. No more than a cheetah knows how it runs so fast. It was innate and unquestioned. If Christian ever gave thought to it, he might be lost in an area of psychology that hadn't yet been explored. Luke could make a pretty good career out of it, but he knew he never would. He was addicted now. To the hunt. To saving people. To...

His *desire.*

Luke kept looking around the bar, ignoring the talk and motion around him. He had to ignore it or go on a murder spree himself, so his mind blocked it all out the way a painter can sit at an easel for hours without glancing up.

Luke's easel was this bar, and his painting was Christian. The boy's problem wasn't his hunch but his tactics. He moved through the establishment like a machine, walking from one end of the place to the other. He moved slow, taking in everything, but his mind was going too fast. Dismissing too much.

Luke had spotted who they wanted. The video they watched in Christian's office had been grainy, but the man had been visible in it. Christian was right. The man was here again. Absurd, making Luke wonder if the man was stupid. His original pattern didn't lend itself to that assessment, but here he was, all the same.

Christian hadn't seen him because the man was doing a decent job of concealing himself.

He was sitting with a young woman at a table for two in the very back of the club's VIP section. He rarely looked out into the crowd and kept his face half hidden.

Christian wouldn't see the man unless he slowed down or barged into VIP. Luke thought it would be the latter. Christian's mind couldn't slow down. It didn't know how.

Luke looked at his scotch before catching a bartender's eye.

"May I have another?"

"Sorry, what?" the woman asked.

"May I have another?" Luke said louder, annoyed that the bar couldn't accommodate him.

The drink arrived, and Luke continued waiting. He wondered what Christian would do when he finally found the man he so desperately wanted.

There was only one area Christian hadn't ventured to. The VIP section. He had tried viewing it from multiple angles, but he couldn't see everything.

Two people in particular were hidden. They sat in a corner, far away from the main floor. The rest of the groups in VIP had multiple people, and all of them moved freely through the roped area and into the main bar. These two hadn't stood, and Christian couldn't get a clear view of the man's face.

Go up there and see, the Other said in his mind.

Christian heard him clearly despite the club's noise. He swallowed, his usual fear rearing despite his mind's dominance. He hadn't used his credentials in a place like this before. He knew he could, but it was foreign.

He shoved the fear down and pulled out his wallet as he approached the entrance closest to him. A large bouncer stood in front of the red velvet rope. He stood 6'2" and dwarfed Christian in every possible way.

"Wristband," the bouncer said without looking at Christian.

He unfolded his wallet and held his FBI identification out to the bouncer. "I'm Special Agent Christian Windsor. I'm working a case. I need access back there."

The bouncer looked down at the wallet, then reached forward and took it. He stared at it for a moment before looking at Christian. "I'm going to need to take it out."

"Okay."

The bouncer pulled the ID out to feel its weight. He flipped it over and looked at the back. "Give me a second." He tilted his head slightly back to his earpiece. "I've got an FBI agent here saying he needs access to VIP—"

"Stop," Christian interjected, his mind grabbing control again. "No one can know I'm in there besides you. Tell whoever is on the other end of that thing that you're mistaken, or you'll be jeopardizing my investigation."

The bouncer stopped talking and eyed Christian again. It took a second, but Christian saw the man's face change.

The bouncer understood he was no longer in charge of the situation. Christian's warning had stopped whatever he'd been about to do. He spoke into his earpiece again. "Never mind. Just someone fucking around." He focused on Christian. "Look, if there's going to be trouble in here, I need to know, and so do the staff."

"There's not going to be any trouble. Most likely, nothing will happen. You watch me from here, and if you see something spark, alert everyone, okay?"

The bouncer nodded slowly. He stepped aside and removed one end of the rope, creating an opening for Christian. "Where are you going to be?"

"On the other side. I'll probably leave once I've surveilled the area. If you see me move toward someone, don't do anything. You understand?"

The bouncer nodded again and let Christian step through.

He immediately found the couple he wanted.

That's him, the Other said. *You know it's him. You know we're right.*

Christian said nothing as he walked across the VIP section, moving by the tables until he reached the opposite end.

It's him, and the woman makes sense, doesn't she? the Other asked. *Young, just like the last one. Look at her. He's really working her. She's in love with him already, and I'd guess he feels the same.*

Christian glanced to his right and saw his replica

standing there, smiling like an evil clown who found joy only in others' suffering.

What are you going to do? the Other asked.

Christian didn't know. He had only hoped he'd see the man here, and there he was, in the flesh and ready to take someone else.

Are you going to call Luke? Maybe tell the bouncer?

Seconds passed slowly. Christian focused on the man, looking at his smile, at the way his eyes held such glee.

I don't think you want to do any of that, the Other continued. *I think you want to kill him right now. You want to force him to make a move and then pull the gun on your hip and put a bullet right in his head.*

"No," Christian said. He knew how foolish it would be to fire a weapon in a place like this. His career would come to a standstill, and an investigation of *him* would follow. As for the moral implications?

What moral implications? the Other said.

"Shut up." Christian wasn't going to entertain the thought.

He turned away from the table and walked back to the bouncer.

"Okay, go ahead and get everyone over here. You see that table in the back? The two people sitting there. I need you to get the man. If you and your colleagues apprehend him, there won't be a scuffle. You got a back room here?"

The bouncer nodded as he looked at the VIP's far side.

"Where is it?"

The bouncer turned and pointed at the club's corner.

"I'll be waiting there for you. Bring him to the room."

Christian turned and walked in the direction the

bouncer had pointed. He didn't see the Other anywhere. He was done talking for now.

Luke smirked as Christian talked to the bouncer again.

It meant he had more work to do. Christian had decided not to do anything dangerous in this place, choosing instead to seize the man almost by the book. Luke knew Christian would call within a few minutes, asking him to show up here.

He finished his scotch and left forty dollars on the bar.

CHAPTER NINE

Christian stood outside the manager's office. Two bouncers stood behind him, and two more were inside the office with the man. As expected, he hadn't put up a struggle.

He'd gotten another bouncer to grab the woman, too. She was being held in the kitchen, the only other place away from the public's eye.

"If you wanted to go out on the town, you could have just told me," Luke said as they entered the hallway.

"He's in there."

"Our man?"

Christian nodded.

"Identification?" one of the bouncers standing next to Christian said.

Luke took out his badge and handed it over without looking. "Why do you think it's him?"

Christian glanced at the closed office door. "I just know."

"I'm sure that will hold up once he asks for a lawyer."

"It's him."

"It's not going to matter," Luke said. "We'll have him for an hour, tops. He's probably accusing the club of false imprisonment right now."

"Well, we'll have his name and where he lives. We'll have everything about him before the night's over."

"Okay," Luke said. "Ready?"

Christian nodded and looked at the bouncer. "Thanks for your help. Have the other guys leave the room once we go in, okay?"

"Do you want us to do anything?" the bouncer asked.

"No. We'll be done within thirty minutes. I'll let you know when we're finished."

"The manager is on his way," the bouncer said. "He's going to want to speak with you."

"That's fine. As soon as I'm done in there. Tell him not to come in or bother us until we're out, okay?"

The bouncer nodded. Christian could tell he didn't like the idea of telling his boss any such thing.

"Let's go," Christian said and opened the door.

Luke followed, and the two bouncers came behind him.

"Guys, they're asking for the room. Rob's gonna be here in a minute," the bouncer said.

Christian assessed the man standing against the wall, seeing his relaxed composure in the way he leaned casually on the wall for the act it was. His hands were in his pockets and he looked at his feet as if he were waiting for a train.

The bouncers closed the door, leaving Christian and Luke alone with the man.

"What's this all about?" he asked, meeting their stares.

"Your ID says your name is Ted Hinson. That right?"

Christian asked, glancing at the identification one of the bouncers had given to him a few minutes previously.

"That's right. Am I being detained?"

"No. Not by us."

"What about the bouncers? Are they detaining me?"

"No bouncers here," Luke said.

"Well, if I'm not being detained, I'd like to leave."

"Who was the woman you were with?" Luke asked.

"Not sure. You should ask her." Hinson straightened up from the wall and faced Christian. "Since I'm not under arrest or being detained, I'm asking to leave. Are you stopping me?"

"No. You're free to leave whenever you'd like," Christian said.

Luke moved to stand in front of the door. Christian heard the lock turn.

"There aren't any cameras in here, Mr. Hinson. It's best that you answer our questions," Luke said.

They had just entered the realm of illegality. Christian felt a brief flare of fear rise in his head. The calm in Luke's voice crushed it.

Hinson smiled. "How do you know I'm not recording this with my cellphone?"

"The bouncers didn't let you take it out of your pocket," Christian said. "I made sure of that before they brought you in. Your ID says you live in Atlanta. Why are you here?"

Hinson looked at his feet, seeming to realize that he would have to play ball for at least a few minutes.

Christian knew they didn't have much time. The club's

owner would be here soon and demand that they let him in.

"Vacation," Hinson said.

"You were here just a week ago, weren't you?" Christian hadn't looked at the man's travel history, but Hinson didn't know that.

Hinson said nothing. Luke moved around to the owner's desk and leaned against it, creating a triangle between the three of them. "What are you doing with the women? Are you killing them? Or are you keeping them?"

"I have no idea what you're talking about. You sound insane."

Christian didn't want the manager having to knock on the door. If Hinson lawyered up later, and the manager was asked, the locked door was evidence of possible false imprisonment.

"I know your name now, Ted Hinson," Luke said. "Theodore Hinson. That's a very regal name. You come from good stock, don't you? Probably attended a lot of affairs when you were younger, maybe listened to your parents talking about the problems all the blacks were causing in our great nation. I'm sure they discussed high tax rates on the rich and how the lower classes needed to pull themselves up by the bootstraps. Did they have any idea what you were turning into?"

Hinson's face was blank.

"I know your name." Luke stood from the desk, obviously thinking the same thing as Christian. He went back to the door and unlocked it, then pulled it open. "You're free to leave. We'll see you again."

The man looked at Luke with the same blank face, not

carefree, not angry, just emptiness. He turned that blank stare on Christian for a second, then the smile returned. "My lawyer will enjoy taking your jobs."

He walked out of the room, leaving the two of them standing alone. A few seconds passed as they watched him walk down the hallway, flanked by bouncers on both sides.

"The owner is in the parking lot," one said to Christian.

"If he does lawyer up, Waverly is going to hear about the whole thing," Tommy said over Christian's speakerphone. "We need to tell him first thing Monday morning."

Christian and Luke had returned to Christian's hotel room in the early hours of Saturday morning. Christian was on the bed, staring up at the ceiling wearing the hotel-provided robe. He was barefoot, while Luke wore his usual shirt and tie and was sitting in a chair with one leg crossed over the other.

"That's fine." They hadn't slept yet, but Christian didn't feel tired. He'd spent all night learning everything he could about Ted Hinson. "He's a professor at the University of Georgia's business school. Terry College of Business. He's tenured and is in accounting. From what I can tell, fifty percent of his time is spent teaching. The other fifty percent is spent on research."

"What the hell do accounting professors research?" Tommy asked.

"Correlations between businesses and outcomes. The markets, et cetera," Luke said.

"All right, I'm trying to think about this like Waverly is going to because the man will claim illegal detainment."

"No proof," Christian said.

"Fine. But Waverly will say you went off a hunch and detained a tenured professor while he was on a date with no physical evidence. With no evidence at all, actually. What are you going to say to him?"

"We need to find some evidence."

"Yeah, well you better make it quick. Did you two get a ticket home already?"

"No, we're going to wait and see what Waverly says Monday. I want to be able to look at him when I have to explain this."

"Jesus Christ, Christian," Tommy said. "Are you sure you know what you're doing here? Because as your partner, it's not looking like it."

Christian kept staring at the ceiling, knowing Tommy was scared for him.

Do I know what I'm doing?

The Other didn't speak to him. He didn't need to. Christian held no doubt in his mind.

"I do. You'll see."

CHAPTER TEN

The meeting with Waverly had gone as expected. Horribly.

Ted Hinson had indeed retained counsel, and by nine in the morning Luke, Christian, and Tommy had all been sitting in Waverly's office.

He'd told them in no uncertain terms that they were to drop the case immediately. That they had fucked up, and he knew they hadn't let the man out of the room when he'd asked to leave.

"Whatever is going on in your head, Christian, don't tell anyone about it unless there's evidence to back it up. You understand?" Waverly had said.

Christian told him he understood.

From now on, he would keep his thoughts to himself. That didn't mean the case was over. Christian hadn't said he understood *that*.

Christian wondered what the shrink had written in his file after their first meeting. He had an idea it read something like:

Patient is depressed. He may be having delusions and may

79

have had them for much of his life. It seems his family supported these hallucinations. The movie, A Beautiful Mind *popularized the notion of the scientist's mind being too powerful to be content with a normal life. Further sessions needed to determine scope and depth. As of now, recommendation is to leave Christian Windsor in the field, pending more sessions.*

Christian knew he wasn't delusional. Or at least, he hadn't been when his mind only projected his mother and Melissa. Now that he saw the Other, he wasn't as sure. He hadn't even brought *that* up to Hanson.

Christian sat in his office with Dr. Hanson on his computer screen in front of him. It was time for his next therapy session.

"Did you hear?" Christian asked.

"No? What happened?"

"Waverly closed down the DC case. He said my hunches were unfounded, and he didn't want to hear anything else unless I had hard evidence."

"I imagine you know the next question I'm going to ask, given your background."

"How does it make me feel," Christian said, but it wasn't a question.

Hanson nodded.

Christian said nothing, his gaze shifting above his computer to avoid the doctor's stare.

"Well?" Hanson asked.

"He's right," Christian lied, looking back at the screen. "If there isn't evidence to back up what I think, then I need to find evidence before I bring something to him."

"Do you really believe that?"

"Why would I lie?"

Hanson smiled. "Christian, I know you're smarter than me. I don't sit in this chair with any delusions about my limitations or your lack of them. The easiest thing you can do in these sessions is to lie to me and tell me what you think the director *wants* to hear. Then you can stop seeing me, and Director Waverly will go on with the rest of his job. I may not be as smart as you, but I'm not easily bull-shitted, either."

"Look, Waverly wants me to follow the foundation of law enforcement. Look for evidence and make arrests when I find it. I agree with that. If I didn't, I would be unfit to be an agent."

"Some part of you," Hanson said, "has to think he's wrong. It's not arrogance to understand how smart you are. It's not arrogance to realize that the rest of the world isn't that smart and may make poor decisions because of it. Yes, the director is right in how law enforcement operates, but it doesn't mean he's right in this case. It doesn't mean you don't realize that, either."

"Do you think he's right?" Christian asked.

"I don't know what you were doing as far as your investigation goes. I have a full caseload myself, and I can't keep up with specific investigations. My job is to help agents maintain steady mental states."

"You've said how smart I am. Do you think he's right that I need evidence, even if my mind tells me I don't?"

"Of course he is right. Evidence is primary. Now, you answer the same question."

Christian looked above his computer. Yes, Waverly was wrong. It was the worst decision Christian had seen him make since joining the FBI. Ted Hinson had taken six women and was about to take his seventh before Christian stepped in.

Mary Lawson didn't know how lucky she was. If they couldn't watch Hinson, he'd do it again. More lives would be lost.

Christian knew he couldn't say any of that. He looked at the screen and said, "He's right. You are, too. Evidence is primary."

A pause ensued, and Christian asked the question he'd been thinking about earlier. "Do you think I'm having delusions?"

"Based on the people you see who aren't actually there?" Christian nodded.

"It's possible. Typically the affected person is delusional because he doesn't realize those things are figments of his imagination. You've told me you know they aren't real, which would mean you're not delusional, but it's still a mental aberration."

"I suppose it is."

"Delusions are when *your* reality doesn't match up with *actual* reality."

"Do you think that's happening with me?"

"I don't know," Hanson said. "Tell me about this investigation that was shut down and what you were thinking."

It had been a while since Christian showed up this late at Luke's house.

He knocked on the door as the storm shook the world around him. Harsh lightning created streaks across the sky in almost constant flashes, and the thunder kept pace. Rain hadn't fallen yet, but it was coming.

Luke opened the door and said nothing as he walked to the living room. Christian stepped in and closed the door, following him across the foyer.

"Coffee?" Luke asked.

"No."

"I think I'll pass tonight, too."

The lights were off overhead and the lightning outside out-shined the moon, becoming the only thing to illuminate the room. Luke sat on his couch. Christian walked to the window and stared outside.

"What brought you here, Christian?"

A day had passed since Christian had met with Hanson. They had a follow-up appointment for next week. They would continue until Waverly was satisfied.

"I'm wondering if I'm losing my mind."

"Why would you think that?"

"Look at what's happening to my life," Christian said. "I have no one anymore, and I may have just ended my career with what happened in DC."

"No need for dramatics. The fact that you can sit in a room with the FBI director whenever you want says a lot."

"Have you ever been reprimanded at work?"

"Once."

"What happened?" Christian asked. The first drops of rain started falling from the sky onto the lawn.

"I came to the FBI."

"So you left?"

"Not because of the chastisement, but yes, I did."

"Why did you leave?"

"We haven't discussed purpose much, have we?"

Christian shook his head.

"I didn't feel my purpose was aligning with either my psychiatric practice or academia. The Sphere was prestigious, but that isn't my purpose."

"Does the FBI line up with it?"

"It's beginning to," Luke said. "Do you have a purpose?"

"I used to. Or at least, I thought I did."

"What was it?"

"What's yours?" Christian replied.

"I asked first."

Christian was quiet for a second. He remembered what he had told Waverly when he was first recruited to this team. The reasoning had been simple.

"I thought I wanted to help people. I wanted to be like my mother. She makes everyone's life better. I thought I could do that here, in my own way."

"Are you not?"

"I've hurt everyone I've gotten close to since I joined," Christian said.

"Have you hurt me?"

"I'm not sure you're capable of being hurt, Luke."

Lightning flashed harshly outside, illuminating the room.

"You don't think I've ever been hurt?"

Like the flash of lightning, clarity came unbidden to Christian. It was as if three-and-a-half years of knowing Luke finally connected in his mind, all the separate pieces lining up to form a picture.

"No. You've never loved anyone, have you, Luke?" Christian turned. "You've lived your life separate from everyone and everything. Even your girlfriend doesn't matter to you, does she?"

"I have loved before. Now, my purpose is what matters to me."

"And what is it?"

Luke stood and walked to the other side of the large bay window. He didn't face Christian but looked out at the night. "Do you believe in God?"

"No."

"Why not?"

"There's no proof. There isn't a wizard in the sky dictating the world."

"What about the idea that God is the great clockmaker? He set this universe up and is letting it run?"

"It's a nice thought," Christian said, "but again, there's no proof."

"I believe in God, Christian. I do not need proof because I have faith. He, or It, exists. That is my purpose."

"God? When was the last time you went to church?"

Luke smiled, and his teeth were pearly white underneath the lightning's glow. "It's more complicated than church." He turned to Christian. "You didn't come here to discuss my purpose. Tell me why you think you're losing your mind. Is the replica of yourself still around?"

Christian nodded.

"What does he say?"

"That Waverly is wrong. That we won't find any evidence, but Hinson will continue taking women. Possibly killing them."

"Is that all?"

"No," Christian said. "He says that I have to keep going, evidence or no evidence."

"Faith, the same as I have in God. You have faith in yourself, in your mind's ability, even if no one else does. I don't see where insanity comes into play."

"And the fact that I see visions?"

"Everyone God spoke to in the Bible could be said to have had visions. Perhaps they did. Perhaps none of it's real, and they're all just stories to keep people faithful. Something that has always struck me, and perhaps Lucy Speckle would have understood this, is that Jesus's disciples died by awful methods. Boiled alive. Crucified upside down, like Lucy nearly did to me. They met the man, Jesus, and they all died for him."

"What are you saying, Luke?"

"Only that faith is a powerful thing. It has started and ended civilizations. No one had proof. They believed, and nothing in the world would stop them. Some people might call it insanity, but I think it's something to be admired. Perhaps even aspired to."

"So... You're saying I should listen to the Other?" Christian knew what he was asking and that Luke's answer could go against Director Waverly's order.

"Your faith has served you well so far, as has mine. I think, for both of us, it would be cosmically foolish to leave our faith now."

CHAPTER ELEVEN

"They won't be bothering you anymore."

"You're sure?" Ted asked.

"Yes. This went all the way up to the FBI director, from what I've heard. The agents who held you have been corrected. No one will be coming to see you."

Ted listened to his lawyer over the phone, but he couldn't shake the way that one man had looked. The older one who leaned against the desk. Luke Titan. Ted knew his name. He had been a rock star in academia. Titan's face had said that nothing was over, and it would never be over until he had what he wanted—Ted Hinson and the family he was creating.

"You there?" his lawyer asked.

"Yes. I'm just not sure, Fred. You weren't in the room. These guys are nuts."

"Trust me, okay? It's over. Just stay out of DC. Don't give them any reason to look at you."

"So I have to restrict my fucking travel?" Ted said.

"No. Just DC. Go anywhere else, but leave DC alone for

a few months. I mean, you don't have to, but it might make things easier. Although, if you *must* go to DC, you'll be fine."

Ted swallowed and nodded. "All right, thanks a lot, Fred."

"No problem. Call me if you need anything."

Ted hung up the phone and leaned back in his office chair. His door was shut, but even so, he had spoken quietly to his lawyer. He didn't want people hearing anything about this, not even a whisper. Ted had been freaking out since Saturday, and it was already Wednesday.

He didn't know how they'd found him, and he couldn't figure it out. He had spent endless hours trying to understand how it was possible, but nothing came to him.

It *wasn't* possible, yet they had been there, and Titan had told him he knew his name.

It still sent chills down Ted's spine.

Another part of him grew angry thinking about Titan wanting to control his family. His ex-wife had already tried that. Wrecked Ted's family. Taken his child from him and the love they had built.

Now *just* when he had something good going for him, this man wanted to steal it.

Ted barely thought about the younger agent. He had been nothing. The real threat rested with Titan.

"You're not going to stop me," Ted said to himself, not hearing the growl in his voice. "You're not going to break up my family."

Ted decided that he would keep going. He needed to change his tactics, but that was fine. His lawyer was good, great even, and if he said the FBI was off his trail, then they were.

I know your name. Titan's voice echoed in his head.

"And I know yours, motherfucker."

He was already two weeks behind schedule. He'd fix it, though.

Tonight.

Ted's original plan had been to find the perfect mixture of wives. He was still using condoms with them. No one was ready for a child yet, although that was his end goal.

What Titan's little interruption had done was show him that he had to choose between perfection or good enough. Ted was going with good enough.

He had driven around Christy's neighborhood for an hour tonight, looking at her house with each pass. The lights were on inside, and a strange car was in the driveway. Ted didn't need to have *Luke Titan's* intelligence to know what that meant.

Another man had been there with his wife and his daughter.

Ted gripped the steering wheel tightly, his knuckles turning a staunch white. He kept driving through the neighborhood until he saw the car leave. He'd looked into the other car as it passed him, but the darkness limited what he could see.

All Ted knew was that a man sat in the driver's seat four feet from him, and he couldn't do a thing about it.

Seven houses down from Christy's, Ted stopped the car.

He looked at the time and saw that it was eleven. The bastard had waited until after Ted's daughter was asleep before leaving. Thinking about someone else around Callie while she was going to bed disgusted him.

Focus, he thought. *You have a plan and you need to follow through with it.*

That was true. Driving around Christy's neighborhood certainly had nothing to do with it. He would deal with her tomorrow, telling her in no uncertain terms that if she had a strange man around his daughter one more time, they would go back to court.

Now, he had to get back on schedule.

Yes, he thought. *Getting on schedule will put everything right.*

Ted left the neighborhood, careful to stick to the speed limit. He pulled out onto the highway and drove toward Atlanta. It was an hour away, but he wanted to get there a bit later.

His mind danced around thoughts of Titan while he drove, mixing in the anger and disgust he felt at Christy. He felt like everything was against him, trying to keep him from finding happiness. When Ted was a child, his mother and father had told him the one thing in this world he should seek was happiness. Now, it was like an unseen deity was sitting behind a curtain, pulling strings to keep him from achieving his birthright.

Ted reached Atlanta and kept heading south. Atlanta proper had some seedy places, but not nearly as ghetto as he wanted.

The streets were dark, with neon lights illuminating the windows of one-story buildings. Storefronts with signage reading PAWN SHOP, or JADE SPA, and everything was capitalized.

It didn't take long to find a prostitute.

She was walking on the road, her skirt nearly showing her entire ass. Ted hadn't envisioned himself taking a wife like this, someone willing to denigrate themselves to make a living. But what was family for if not to help people when they were down? Ted's mother and father had taught him that much.

He pulled the car to a stop right in front of the hooker's path and rolled his window down as she walked over.

"Hey, baby, you need a date?" the woman asked.

Ted looked at her face, and saw she was beautiful, despite the circumstances she'd found herself in. He could help her. He could change all of this for her.

"Sure," he said. "Want to get in?"

"You're not a cop are you?"

"Ha! No way."

The prostitute looked at him for a moment, deciding whether or not to believe the white man that had somehow found himself in this part of town.

"Two hundred for an hour," she said.

"No problem. Wanna get in?"

"Sure, baby," the woman said and walked to the passenger side of the car.

Ted unlocked the door, and she got in. "You got a room around here?" he asked.

"Yeah. Pull out here and take a right."

"How's your night going?" Ted asked as he followed her directions. His left hand reached unobserved between his legs for the knife he'd been riding with for hours.

"Ain't bad."

The prostitute didn't offer any other conversation as Ted continued driving down the road.

She eventually said, "Take a right."

Ted did, and as her eyes followed the car's lead, he whipped her in the temple with the butt of the knife.

The prostitute didn't even turn her head. She slumped to her right, her head smacking against the window. It was the only sound she made.

Ted kept driving, calm despite the unconscious woman next to him. It took him about five minutes to find a deserted lot. He worked quickly to transfer the woman to his trunk.

He stared down at her, the trunk's light showing him whom he was adding to his family. She was so gorgeous. He could barely believe it. Far prettier than any of his other wives.

Perhaps he had been wrong to only go after middle and upper-class women. Perhaps what he needed was a lady of the night to liven things up.

CHAPTER TWELVE

Veronica parked her car across the street from the Atlanta FBI headquarters. A week had passed since her last appointment with Luke, and she couldn't shake what he'd said. She didn't know how badly this would end, but regardless, she was going inside.

Christian needed help.

She had told herself over and over that she wasn't going to reach out. That she wouldn't be the one to extend a hand. Truthfully, she didn't fully understand her feelings toward Christian.

Their relationship had been brief, at least compared to some of Veronica's past ones. It had been physical, but that wasn't *it*. She'd had physical relationships before, but if her mind was a beach that Christian held sway over, those other lovers didn't amass to a single grain of sand.

Veronica walked through the FBI entrance and into the lobby. She went to the front desk, where a young, black man in a suit was sitting.

"Hi, I have an appointment with Christian Windsor."

"Your name?"

"Veronica Lopez."

The man looked at his computer screen for a few moments, then said, "I don't see your name here."

"Could you call him? I'm sure he'll confirm our appointment." Veronica was sure of no such thing. Most likely, he'd turn her away.

The man picked up the phone and punched in a few numbers.

"Hi, Special Agent Windsor. This is Theo Lawrence with security. I have a Veronica Lopez here. She says she has an appointment with you, but I don't see it on the visitor list. Did you forget to add her?"

Another pause and Veronica felt her heart beating inside her ears. She was so nervous that this would be another rejection in her futile quest to just make contact.

"Yes, sir," the man said. He put the phone down and looked at Veronica. "He forgot to put you on the list. Let me print you an ID badge and you can go on up."

It took another moment. Then the security guard handed her the badge. "Do you know where his office is?"

"Yes. Thanks a lot."

Veronica turned and went to her right, heading to the elevator. She went up to the sixth floor and stepped off, stopping when she came in sight of Christian's office.

He was sitting behind the computer. It'd been six months since they had last seen each other. She realized she looked like the clichéd crazy ex-girlfriend, showing up at his place of work to beg him to take her back.

That's not true, she told herself. *You're not here to beg.*

You're here to see how bad he's doing. You're here to try and help if you can.

Veronica started walking again, heading to her lost lover's office.

Luke glanced up at the perfect time and smiled at what he saw. He was usually very careful to mask his feelings, but the smile slipped by his defenses.

Veronica Lopez looked frightened, but that didn't matter. She was here, and Luke felt a surge of pride in her. She was going the extra mile, showing up at the boy's place of work.

Maybe you do *belong with the three of us,* he thought. *Your will is fairly impressive, Ms. Lopez.*

Luke leaned back in his chair and watched her walk around the inner office cubicles. His conversations with Christian had been fruitful, and adding this to the mix… It was all superb.

Ted Hinson could go on killing people. Luke was fine with that. Ted would end up dead, and the women he took held no significance for Luke's plan.

Corrupting Christian Windsor was all-important, and Luke had to admit that things were going swimmingly.

Veronica didn't pause outside Christian's door to gather herself. She knew he had seen her. She knocked and waited for him to let her in.

Christian opened the door. "Lying to federal officers is a crime."

"He's a security guard, not a federal officer." Veronica walked in, not waiting for him to move and give her entrance.

Christian lithely stepped aside as Veronica walked to the conference table. He shut the door. "Why are you here?"

"When was the last time you talked to your mom?" she asked.

Christian went over to his desk and sat. Veronica remained standing.

"If you're going to be here, at least keep up appearances and have a seat. You have an appointment with me, after all."

Veronica knew he was right. She didn't want to cause him problems or make things uncomfortable with his job. She took the seat in front of his desk. "Answer my question. When was the last time you talked to your mom?"

"I don't know. Four days, maybe."

"It's been a week, Christian. I called her last night. She said you're only calling once a week now."

Christian turned his chair around and looked out the window.

Veronica knew why. He hated eye contact during important conversations. He had done this when he first told her he liked her, sitting at that restaurant over a year ago. The conversation had been different back then. Very, very different.

"Why aren't you calling her?"

"You know the answer."

"I know you're not well, Christian."

Veronica didn't know what was going on in his head. She could never grasp the inner workings of this man she loved, and before, she had been fine with that. Now, she *needed* to understand. "Talk to me. If just this once. You think this has been easy on me? The only thing I wanted when I got out of that fucking storage unit was to be with *you*. I wanted to help you heal and thought you'd do the same for me. But neither of us is healing."

"I don't know how much more succinctly I can say it, Veronica. The people I'm close to get hurt."

"Then quit this fucking *job*. You told me you joined the FBI to help people, but if helping strangers means you have to hurt those you love, it's not the right place to be."

"I can't quit," he said.

"Why not?"

"Because more people will die if I leave. A lot more."

"What do you owe them, Christian? Do you owe them your own life? Your happiness?"

"I don't know, but I don't owe them yours."

"Goddammit, turn around and look at me," Veronica said.

The chair spun slowly, and he sank deeper into it, like a teenager sitting in the back of class.

"I didn't come here to ask you to date me," she said. "I came because I'm worried. Your mother is nearly out of her mind, but she won't say anything to you about it. She'll keep acting like everything's fine because she doesn't want to put more stress on you."

Christian was quiet for a second, then as if she hadn't spoken, he said, "How are you?"

Veronica laughed. "Me?" She didn't know how to answer. She hadn't been thinking about herself when deciding to come here. It had all been about him. "I don't know. I mean, I'm better than I was. I still have nightmares about Speckle. I have nightmares about you, too. I'm better, but I'm not good, Christian."

"I'm so sorry." Tears filled his eyes.

"*You* didn't do *any* of this. At least not the parts involving Speckle and Brown. You only own how *you* treat people, but I don't think that's what you're apologizing for."

He just looked at her.

"I can live with the things that have happened to me." Her words were flowing now, things she had wanted to say for so long but hadn't been able to. Months of pain and thought all erupted from the place where she had buried them.

"If they happened to me as a child, I'd probably be a lot more messed up, but I'm not a child. I'm an adult. The dreams won't go away, but I'll keep living. I'll keep trying to be happy. I don't even know why I love you like this. Any other man, I would have let them go with hardly a thought. But you… I can't just quit, Christian. Looking at you now…" Tears came to her eyes. "You're not well. You need help."

She saw him fighting to keep from crying, but Veronica couldn't. She reached up and wiped her right eye as a tear spilled from it.

"I can't do this right now," he said.

"Then when can you? I was letting you go, as much as it hurt me. But seeing you now, I can't. Not until I know you're okay, even if that's not with me. So if I have to camp in your yard, I'll do it until you get a restraining order, Christian."

He went quiet again and looked over the top of her head, avoiding her gaze. Ten seconds passed with her staring at him, watching him try to control his emotions.

"Come by tonight," Christian finally said.

"When?"

"Eleven."

Veronica looked on for a bit longer, though his eyes still didn't venture down. "Okay."

She wanted to say, *I love you*, but didn't. Instead, she stood and left the office.

Luke waited ten minutes after Veronica left before picking up his phone and dialing her number.

"Hello?"

"It's Luke. I'm calling from my office line. I saw you talking to Christian. How are you feeling?"

"Not good," she said, sniffling. "I'm sitting in my car, crying."

"I'm sorry. What did he say?"

"Well, that's the only bright spot. He said I could come over tonight."

"Are you going to go?" Luke asked.

"Yeah." She sniffed again.

"That's good. If you need to talk, call me, Veronica. You don't have to wait for our next appointment."

"Thanks, Luke."

"Okay. Talk soon. Bye."

Luke hung up the phone and glanced across the floor at Christian's office. The boy was gone. Luke imagined his emotions were very similar to Veronica's right now.

The lovers would reunite tonight. Luke looked back at his computer screen, the smile covering his face again.

COURTSHIP

CHAPTER THIRTEEN

Sarah Yields was sitting in front of Ted. She couldn't imagine what she looked like after months spent in darkness, unshaven and unkempt.

She wasn't concerned with her looks because *he* could see her. She didn't care what this madman thought of her. She didn't know why she'd thought about her appearance at all. Perhaps it was because this was the first time she'd been led upstairs.

Ted had brought home another woman. Sarah didn't know how long ago. A day? Two? Three? Days were a concept from a past life that no longer held meaning.

Sarah was frightened despite the brief concern for her appearance, which she knew to be a damned stupid thing to worry about. She was frightened because she didn't know if Ted was finally going to rape her.

"What do you think of Chanice?" Ted said.

Sarah almost laughed. Maybe all the suffering over the past few months hadn't fully destroyed her personality. This man had kidnapped multiple women, killed one, and held the rest captive, and now he was asking her opinion on his newest conquest like she was a new coworker and he wanted to make sure she was fitting in.

"It's okay," he said. "You can talk to me. You're different than the others. I do care about them deeply. Perhaps... I don't know. Perhaps my methods have made them a bit less honest with me. I think you'll be honest. That's why I brought you up here tonight."

Well, that's just great, Ted, because at first I thought you were going to rape me like you do the others. I'm glad you think I'm an honest person. It means a lot.

She knew why he was asking. The woman downstairs had talked to Sarah while Ted was gone. Somehow he had thought that kidnapping a prostitute was a good idea. Ted didn't have a lot of experience with women who had turned to that kind of life. Sarah knew "turn" wasn't the appropriate word. "Had been forced into that kind of life" was more accurate.

Sarah had experience with them, and maybe that was another reason Ted had brought her upstairs. She didn't remember their first conversation fully. Too many drinks had been involved, but she must have told him she was a social worker.

Prostitutes were—and Sarah would never say this in front of colleagues since it would have been a major faux pas—broken people. They would see more and hurt more in twenty years than others would in multiple lifetimes.

Chanice was living proof of that.

She hadn't screamed at Ted. She hadn't begged him to release her. She had cursed him up and down and told him when she got out, she was going to shove his balls down his motherfucking throat, and Sarah wasn't para-phrasing.

"Sarah? I need you to answer me."

"What do you mean, what do I think?"

"You've seen how she's behaving. I hated what I had to do to Keely. I really did. That's not what I want here, for any of you. I can't wait until I can bring you all up here without having to keep you in chains."

He glanced at the cuffs on Sarah's wrists and ankles. She didn't know where the bastard had gotten them from, but he was lucky he had. If he ever let her upstairs without them like he planned to do, she would be out of the first door or window she saw.

"I don't want to hurt Chanice, but I might have made a mistake in bringing her here," Ted finished.

So that was the question: should he kill the prostitute he had beaten and kidnapped? He wanted Sarah to make the decision for him.

"I don't think you should hurt her," Sarah said.

"I'm going to need your help, then. The other women, they aren't in any position to talk sense into Chanice, but you are. I think you're going to be the leader in our house-hold, Sarah. If you want, you can be the matriarch."

Sarah tried to keep her eyes from widening. A matri-arch? A household? She had thought this was more or less a rape factory, but she was learning differently.

Quickly now. Don't dawdle on what this psycho says.

"What do you want me to do?" she asked.

"Talk to her. Tell her it'll be best for everyone if she starts behaving. I'm going to let Marie come up soon to stay. I think she's ready. I'd like to bring another up a little bit after that, but I don't think you're quite ready yet. You will be soon, I hope."

Sarah stared at the man, disbelief filling her mind. He was serious. He wanted to use the women he kidnapped to create a fucking family. He thought it was possible and that *she* would help him.

Sarah swallowed. "I'll talk to her."

"Thank you, Sarah. I appreciate that. You've been much better lately, and I'm going to start treating you much better, too."

Sarah was led back down into the basement. Ted shackled her to the wall, then removed the cuffs he'd used to take her upstairs.

He was close enough for Sarah to do some damage, but she knew it would come to nothing. If she tried hurting him now, whatever trust he had placed in her would vanish, and she couldn't do enough to *actually* hurt him.

Instead, she let him go without saying anything and sat in her designated spot.

He went back upstairs and shut the door, leaving them all in darkness. Chanice had kept quiet and thank God for it.

"Did he fuck you?" she said once the door had closed.

"No."

"You couldn't get out?"

"No. You saw what I was in."

"Jesus, girl. You shoulda at least tried."

Sarah sighed. "Trust me. There wasn't anything I could do."

"That motherfucker ever gets that close to me, he's going to be missing both eyes."

Sarah was quiet for a few minutes, thinking about what he had told her. Chanice's life rested in Sarah's hands. Hadn't that been the real point of the whole conversation? To remove the blame from himself if he killed her because he had asked Sarah very nicely to help him control Chanice?

So now you're the matriarch, and it's your job to keep this family in order.

"Listen to me for a second, okay?"

Chanice was quiet. Sarah took that to mean she'd listen. She had known people who grew up like Chanice most likely had, and they rarely took advice well. Sarah had to try.

"He's going to kill you if you don't stop. He did it to the last woman, who sat right where you are now. He hit her in the head with a mallet. I don't know what he did with the body after he dragged it up those stairs, but she's gone."

"I wish he would," Chanice said.

Sarah thought she heard some fear in her voice and hoped it was enough to save her life. "He will. I don't know what's going to happen to us, but if you want a chance of making it out alive, you need to be quiet. Just let him talk when he comes down. That's all he's done with me so far. Just talks. He's smart, and he's not going to rape you until he thinks it's safe. Until he thinks you're broken. If you want a chance, that's when you'll get it. When he thinks you're his."

"What about all these other bitches in here? They just let him rape them?"

Sarah didn't know what to say about the other women. They all sat in the same darkness, but none of them ever said a word. They were broken. They were his. His will had outlasted theirs, and Sarah wasn't even sure they could be considered human anymore. They were closer to pets. It broke her heart to think it, but she had to be honest with herself if she wanted a chance to escape.

"I don't know, Chanice. I don't know anything about them. You know as much as I do. The answers they give you are the same that they give me, absolutely nothing. All I'm sure of is that if you don't keep quiet, you're going to die."

CHAPTER FOURTEEN

Christian opened the front door and looked at Veronica. He had left work early for the first time in months because he'd told her to show up at eleven, and here she was, right on time.

"Hey," he said.

"Hey."

They both stood there, her on the stoop and him just inside the house.

"You going to let me in?"

"I don't want to."

"Move," Veronica said and walked inside, leaving him standing at the door as she made her way to the kitchen.

Christian shut the door and followed. He knew what she wanted.

"I didn't think you'd touch it," she said as she opened the cabinet to the right of the sink. She pulled down one of the bottles of wine she had brought over when they'd first started dating. She used to drink while they watched television. Christian had never poured himself a glass.

Veronica didn't speak as she moved to the drawers and pulled out a bottle opener. Then she went to another cabinet and grabbed a glass, and finished by pouring the wine.

She drank half in one gulp, then turned to look at him. "I needed that."

"Sometimes I feel like I do, too," Christian said. He stood at the kitchen door, unable to stop the feelings rising in him. Watching the way she moved, how she took over his kitchen as if it was hers. He loved her.

But you always knew that. You did all this because *you loved her.*

"You want a glass?"

Christian shook his head. Neither of them moved. Christian didn't know what to say. He didn't know why he had told her to come over. It had come out of his mouth like so many other things, unbidden.

But she was here, and he didn't have a clue what to say.

"What's happening to you?" she asked.

It took a few seconds, but Christian answered honestly. "I don't know."

"Why did you ask me to come over?"

"I don't know that, either."

"Can we sit down? Can we talk? Please?"

Christian swallowed. Everything he had worked for over the past year was being undone right now. His focus on removing anyone from his life that he could hurt was about to crash around his head.

Christian nodded.

"Come on." She didn't reach for his hand as she walked into the living room.

Christian went along, sitting on the opposite end of the couch from her. He stared at the blank television. He hadn't even bothered turning on a light.

"If you don't want to talk, I have plenty to say."

The glass of wine sat on the table in front of them, and though Christian wasn't looking at Veronica, he felt her eyes on him. "Go ahead."

"My mom told me a long time ago that you don't get married until you can't live without someone. It made a lot of sense at the time. It still does. I'm not proposing to you, but I've been through two *horrible* experiences. Things I never thought possible, that I thought only happened in movies."

She laughed as if still unable to believe it. "I think I can live without you, Christian. Actually, I know I can. My mom didn't think about the flip side of her saying, though. The inverse of it. That's what I'm saying to you now. I can live without you, but after everything that's happened, I know that I'm willing to die if it means I can be with you."

All the tears that Christian had held in earlier could no longer be kept at bay. They fell down his face, blurring the dark living room. He didn't know how long he cried or how long it took for Veronica to come to him, but she did.

She wrapped him in her arms, and he let her.

Long ago, Luke had wired Christian's house. He had thought about doing the same to Tommy's, but the risk wasn't worth the reward. At least, not yet. Tommy was in play, of course, but he was a bit player, not the star. Christian was the leading man, and Luke needed to understand everything he could about the boy.

So, he had done the only logical thing. He'd put cameras and microphones in Christian's house. It had been easy enough to place them in each room. He had put the cameras where they gave him maximum visibility, but wouldn't be found without a serious scan of the house. He'd placed microphones in vents and other out of the way places.

He wanted to hear everything that was said in Christian's home.

For the past few years, nothing of importance had happened. The brief relationship between Veronica and Christian had created conversation, but nothing substantial. Luke had never spied on their intimate moments. Everyone needed some privacy.

He had heard Christian's conversations with his mother, although their frequency had decreased greatly in the past few months.

Last night had been filled with a tremendous amount of information, all of it useful.

Luke had listened to Christian cry and watched as Veronica consoled him. He'd waited through that and listened more as they spoke.

He had to be careful with Veronica. He hadn't realized that before last night. He'd underestimated the power she held over Christian. Luke knew how much she loved the boy, but Christian's reciprocation of the feeling was perhaps magnified due to his neurodivergence.

Luke didn't worry. He only needed to be careful. Veronica Lopez might have the power to bring Christian out of his winter, bathing him in rays of sunshine and bringing warmth into the icy landscape he now lived in. Luke just had to make sure that didn't happen.

Today, Luke was out of the office and in the Georgia sunshine. He stood next to his car, parked on North Story Road. In a very rare move for him, he took off his cufflinks and rolled up his sleeves, allowing the sun to hit his arms. Sitting inside his office all day, he enjoyed the opportunity to absorb some vitamin D.

He looked down at his phone and hit call before putting the phone to his ear.

"Terry College of Business. How may I direct your call?"

"Ted Hinson, please."

"Certainly, one second," the receptionist said.

Luke listened to the hold music for a moment. Then he heard Dr. Hinson's voice on the line.

"Ted Hinson."

Luke ended the call and placed the phone back in his pocket.

He looked across the street at Dr. Hinson's house. The neighborhood was older but very nice. Expensive, if not rising to Luke's level.

Luke crossed the street and went up the walkway to the front door. He reached into his pocket and pulled out the two thin utensils he needed to gain entrance. As he had done when he'd killed John Presley, Luke had applied invisible glue to his fingertips to mask his fingerprints. He'd brought nothing else. He only planned on observing.

He turned and checked the street. He absorbed every

minute detail, his mind looking for any movement—especially from inside the other houses.

The only thing he saw were insects living out their lives on perfectly kept lawns.

Luke turned back and stuck the lockpicks into the keyhole. It only took seconds for the pins to click home. He placed the tools back in his pocket and turned the doorknob, then walked inside Ted Hinson's home.

The lights were off, but Luke saw everything perfectly. He took in the smell of the house. He picked up traces of sweat and dirt. Blood, too, and the emotions each carried—primarily fear—moving across the air-conditioned foyer.

Luke went through the house like a ghost, making no noise and leaving no trace. The smells led him to a locked door. Other rooms resided off the hallway, but what he wanted to see wasn't inside them. No, the dirt, sweat, and fear originated behind this door.

A padlock was attached to a small clasp on the door, confirming Luke's thought that Mr. Hinson held something valuable behind it.

Luke pulled his utensils from his pocket again and worked them into the padlock. Once it was open, he removed it, then opened the door on the staircase beyond. He took the first step down, closing the door behind him. He paused, letting his senses take in the room below.

He heard people breathing. From the patterns, he thought there were six women below. Mr. Hinson hadn't even paused and had kidnapped another woman.

Once Luke's eyes had adjusted to the darkness, he walked down the stairs, stopping just before he reached the floor. He saw more in darkness than other people, although not as much as nocturnal animals, much to his chagrin. His retinas could pick up very small amounts of light, allowing him to see great detail.

He didn't step onto the floor. He didn't want the women seeing too much of him.

A white woman sat about ten feet from him, chained to the wall. Luke looked to his right and saw another woman. This one was black. As he looked farther, he saw one more. There was a larger gap between her and the black woman than the first two.

Even Luke couldn't see into the rest of the room. The women on the other side were hidden from him.

Their respiratory rate had increased at least four-fold since he'd descended the stairs. He couldn't hear their heartbeats, but he knew they had probably doubled.

He looked at the floor beneath the black woman and saw traces of blood. Luke could smell the remnants of the bleach that had been used to clean it up.

The black woman's face was bruised, her leg eye swollen shut. Blood crusted her nose, as well. The stain wasn't from her. Mr. Hinson wasn't concerned with his victims' cleanliness, at least not from what Luke could see.

"Ted?" the woman directly in front of Luke said. "Is that you?"

Her question confirmed they couldn't see him, which was good.

Luke walked back up the stairs and went into the main house. He made his way through the hallway, checking the rooms like a person hoping to buy the place. He found the master bedroom and looked it over.

He could smell Hinson. The other women, too. Hinson had brought them here.

Do you fuck them, Mr. Hinson, or do you make love? What do you call it?

Luke went to the bathroom and looked through the medicine cabinet. The usual staples of Tylenol and shaving necessities. He saw no trace of antidepressants or other medications.

"Perhaps they might help," Luke said with a smile.

He went to the living room. The entire house was neatly kept. The furniture was well picked, though not what Luke would have chosen. Taste could run a gamut, however.

"This is good, Dr. Hinson. This will work just fine," Luke said to the empty room.

Two and a half weeks had passed since Christian had last seen Melissa.

She opened the door and motioned for him to enter. "How are you?" she asked as he entered her office.

Christian said nothing in return as he sat on his corner of the couch.

"That's a nice entry," Melissa said.

"I'm about as well as I was last time. Probably worse if I stop and think about it."

"Thinking is overrated," she said, smiling. "Except for one thing, did you think about the question I asked you last time? What do you want to get out of this?"

Christian had known she would begin with it, and he *had* thought about it. *A lot.*

When he'd left here over two weeks ago, he'd believed Melissa would tell him soon that their sessions needed to stop. Perhaps she would recommend someone else, or maybe she would let him go into the world alone. She didn't know about the FBI-assigned psychologist yet. That might even make the whole thing a bit easier.

"I don't know what I want anymore, Melissa, and that's the truth. I used to. I used to be almost singularly focused on what I wanted in life and what I wanted here. I started coming here so you could help me relate to people. I used to want to make people's lives better. Now, I don't know if either of those is true."

"Why are you confused?"

"I'm being pulled in two directions. I don't know. I guess people always have a choice, don't they? Whether you do what's right or wrong. What you want, or what is better for someone else. I don't think I ever really saw life in those terms before, but now I have two options. To do what is right or to do what I want."

"I'm not understanding, Christian. Are you talking about Veronica?" Melissa said.

"Yes and no." He looked down at his feet. "There's someone kidnapping women. He's taking them from multiple states, and I *know* who he is. I don't have any evidence, though, and Waverly ordered me to drop it."

"I see."

"Luke suggested that I ignore Waverly. He thinks I should keep going after this man if I believe he's kidnapping women."

"Luke said that?" Melissa's eyebrows rose.

Christian nodded.

"He's telling you to break the law?"

"I wouldn't necessarily be breaking any laws, only directives from my boss."

"What did you think when Luke said that? Not right now, but your first reaction," Melissa asked.

"I thought he was right. I still think he's right." He looked at his psychiatrist. "If that man is killing people, and I can stop him, why shouldn't I? Because someone who has a title told me differently? On a professional level, the only control he has over me is what I grant him, and I only grant it because he's the director."

"Our world is built on titles, Christian. From policemen to plumbers. All of our positions allow the world to keep running. If you just start ignoring them and do what you want, society will push back."

"You asked what I thought," Christian said.

"Fair enough. Maybe I should ask what you plan to do?"

"Waverly assigned me to a department psychologist," Christian said, ignoring Melissa's question.

Her eyebrows rose again. "He did?"

Christian nodded. "He's concerned about my mental stability."

"So you're cheating on me?" Melissa said, a slight smirk on her face.

"No need to be jealous. I lie to him."

"Why?"

"Because if I tell the truth, I'm not sure I'll be working at the FBI much longer," Christian said.

"But you're not telling the truth in here, either, are you? Not the whole of it."

"I'm not sure I know the truth any longer."

Christian left Melissa's office, lighting a cigarette as soon as he hit the building's front door. He was tired of talking to people. So many, all the time, each one wanting to know the same things.

Everyone except Luke. He was the only person that held a different opinion.

Prerogative, another part of Christian said, although it was whispered and went unheard.

Christian took a drag on the cigarette, not slowing down as he passed the smoking area. He had requisitioned one of the FBI vehicles this morning and was planning on finishing the cigarette inside, despite regulations.

Christian rarely drove, but he was done talking to people. He wasn't going back into his mansion. Luke was right. He had said as much to Melissa, even if she didn't think he would act on it.

He was going to, though. He had decided last night that Hinson must be stopped.

Christian started the vehicle and rolled down the windows to blow his cigarette smoke outside.

He wasn't going to think about Veronica today or what had happened between them last night. He couldn't begin processing that right now. When he'd woken this morning and she was still next to him, he'd kissed her lips briefly before leaving for work.

That was all he could give her until this was done.

Christian had decided something else after they had made love.

His career was over. *That* made the Hinson issue much easier because Waverly firing him didn't matter. Christian wouldn't quit until Ted Hinson was apprehended. Or dead. He didn't care which. Only, this route meant he was done at the FBI.

Christian drove the cruiser from Atlanta to Athens. It was a smallish college town with a lot of money. The poverty was contained in a three-neighborhood area locals called the Iron Triangle. Pizza shops wouldn't even deliver inside it.

Christian had done his research over the past few nights, learning everything he could about Ted Hinson and the college he worked at.

Ted Hinson was divorced with a daughter. His ex-wife Christy and their daughter Callie lived in Athens. The mother had primary custody, and from what Christian gathered, Ted didn't fight it.

A much more detailed report on Hinson resided in Christian's mind, but he wouldn't go to it. He didn't want to know this man, and he had no need for huge, logical leaps in the case. He knew Hinson's address, and that was enough.

He parked across from Ted Hinson's house, not knowing that Luke had done the same thing only hours before. He didn't cross the street as Luke had. He didn't even exit the car. He'd seen the house on Google Maps the previous night, but he wanted to see it in person.

Two stories, with a well-maintained lawn. A large

porch with white rocking chairs adorned the front. It looked like the perfect upper-middle-class suburban home.

Except for the five or more women imprisoned inside. Dead or chained up. Maybe both.

The two windows on the second story stared at him like eyes, as if they knew what he was doing in their neighborhood and didn't like it.

This is our place, and you're not welcome. Go away, lawman. Go away, you pseudo-priest. You bring only false righteousness, and this house will not tolerate it. We will not stop.

Christian heard the house speaking, its voice filling up the car.

Is this a delusion? he wondered. *Is this what Dr. Hanson is afraid of?*

Because he wasn't imagining the house speaking to him. He *heard* it.

Then leave, lawman. Go home where you can't hear us speak anymore. Leave us be.

Christian thought he should feel fear, feel *something*, but he only stared at the talking house with an odd indifference. Perhaps he was hallucinating, or maybe this was another piece of his extrasensory perception. Neither mattered. He had something to do, and when he was finished, he didn't think much would matter anymore.

So let the house talk. Let everything talk. Christian was focused.

He rolled the window up and drove down the road. He had another stop to make before finishing the day. Christian drove across town and parked his car in front of Christy Mackenrow's house.

There were no vehicles in the driveway, just like at Hinson's home.

Christian listened, but this house didn't speak.

Christian got out of the car and slowly walked across the street and up the driveway. He went to the front door and placed his hand on the knob, but he didn't turn it.

Christian closed his eyes and focused on the cold metal beneath his hand. He stood like that for a few seconds, listening to the neighborhood's silence and the soft creaks from inside the house.

Finally, he opened his eyes and returned to his car.

One more place to go.

<hr>

Christian was sitting on a bench on the university's North Campus. It was beautiful, even to Christian's poor sense of design and taste. Buildings surrounded the inner quad, which held green grass, white concrete walkways, as well as fountains.

Christian sat on a stone bench and scrutinized the building on the quad's opposite side.

Ted Hinson would exit shortly, done for the day. Christian wore a baseball cap and a pair of sunglasses. He didn't want to be seen. Waverly couldn't know about this, and if Hinson spotted him, his lawyer would be on the phone within the hour.

Christian wanted one last look at the man before he started in earnest. Luke had been right, even if no one else thought so.

Faith. What else did Christian have any more besides

faith in his mind? Nothing. He'd thrown the rest away. Now, his world *was* his mind, and to not trust it, to not put *faith* in it, was like having no world at all.

Waverly would learn that Christian was right, and he could be done with Christian publicly if needed. Christian didn't care.

Hinson walked out of the building with a messenger bag hung over his shoulder. He took a right once he reached the bottom of the stairs. Christian stood from his bench and followed. The sun shone across the quad, although it was fading as the day grew long.

Hinson didn't look back as he kept walking farther north.

Christian wondered whether he would walk home, drive, or take the bus. He couldn't imagine someone like Hinson getting on a bus with the city's riffraff. His house was only about a mile away. With weather like this, the chances were high that he walked, which Christian preferred. He would only have this chance to be near Hinson. The next time they met, the man would be detained or killed.

Why do you want to get near to him? the Other asked without making an appearance.

Christian did not answer. He didn't need the Other. His mind was made up, and anyone else's input would only confuse him.

It's Veronica, isn't it? That's the reason you decided to go ahead with this. Because last night, you realized a life with no one isn't a life at all. That's sweet, Christian. It is. I'm sure she'd certainly appreciate the sentiment.

The problem, as I see it, is that you're not going to be able to come back. Not fully. Not to the man she first fell in love with. She fucked you last night, but how well does she know you now, Christian? How well does your mother? Luke's winter is real and you're deep inside it, with snow storming all around you. You can't see a path out even if you want to imagine you can. That's the real delusion.

Christian ignored the speech. He looked ahead at Hinson, memorizing his gait. The man didn't look at the stunning buildings surrounding him. Perhaps he'd seen them too many times to take notice. Or perhaps he had other thoughts on his mind.

Thoughts about what was waiting at home.

Hinson walked across the main street, which meant that he wasn't driving. Christian had to stop at the crosswalk, but he kept his eyes on Hinson and picked up his pace when he was allowed to walk again.

Hinson took a left, and so did Christian. The neighborhood was a block up on the right. Christian wouldn't follow any farther. He'd seen all he could without being caught, and he was done looking now.

It was time to use his mind for the FBI one last time— even if it meant breaking all the rules.

CHAPTER FIFTEEN

"Hey."

Luke looked up from his computer. He'd been lost in thought, so much so that he hadn't seen Tommy approaching. Unusual for him and a sign of how deep inside of himself he'd been.

"Hello, Tommy." Luke's face showed nothing of the annoyance he felt at being interrupted.

He had been planning important things. Ted Hinson's situation was much more complex than either Bradley Brown's or Lucy Speckle's had been. Luke was using a good bit of brainpower in figuring out how to operate around the man, despite Waverly's cease and desist order, and now Tommy was here, most likely with another useless conversation.

"Did you look at the email from Roger this morning?"

Luke hadn't opened any emails yet, and he would have put the pathologist's at the end of the line.

"No."

"He's got a body he says we'll want to look at."

"Why?"

"It appears to be a ritualistic killing."

"Religious?" Luke asked.

"No, cultist. The email said it appears to be Satanic."

"Are you going to him now?"

"Yeah," Tommy said. "He asked if we could show up at 3:00, and it's 2:50 already. You coming?"

Luke looked across the hall at Christian's office. It was empty, as it had been all day. Yesterday, too.

"Haven't seen him, either. I didn't even bother calling. Did you?" Tommy asked.

Luke shook his head. He was giving Christian space, or at least the appearance of it. Christian had been at home last night, alone. No phone calls. No talking. He'd stayed up late working from his computer, and Luke realized his error in not tracking *that* as well.

He'd made a mental note to do it soon, although it might prove difficult.

So many challenges, so little time.

"Well, you want to go with me, or you going to stay here?"

"I'll go," Luke said. He stood and grabbed his blazer off the chair. He wasn't interested in the body. He thought he had figured out Tommy's place in all this, and, well, it was grand.

Luke needed to stay close to Tommy. He would be the glue that held their small group together over the next few weeks until everything finally exploded.

If everything went to plan, Luke would even land a large promotion. His ascent wouldn't stop once Christian and Tommy were out of his life. They were stepping stones to grander plans, although Luke couldn't deny they were very *large* stones.

The two were quiet as they approached the elevator and rode down to the building's basement. The term "basement" might sound depressing to an outside observer, but Roger held complete dominion over his floor, directing interns this way and that like a god on Mount Olympus. The man had a nice gig set up for himself.

The elevator stopped, and the two exited, turning toward Roger's main room.

"Right on time," the pathologist said as the two entered. "This is an interesting case. Haven't seen a body like this since the nineties when cults were all the rage."

"Think they're making a comeback?" Tommy said.

"Too soon to tell."

Roger led them to the metal table where the body was prepped for autopsy. "Okay, look here, and here."

Luke listened on autopilot, taking everything in. His mind was far too busy with the current case. The one in which Christian Windsor was lying on this table, even if no one else could see it yet.

FOR CHRISTIAN WINDSOR

Dear Christian,

I have a few more letters left to write, I feel. The things I want to say are fully formed, but I find myself needing to be in a mood for writing, and that takes longer than I'd like. I suppose it works out for the best in our relationship. It has taken quite a long time to arrange things perfectly, and had I written everything early on... Well, who knows if events would have gone the same?

I'm going to give you a choice, Christian. Certainly, it isn't one you ever thought you'd have to make, but you will have a choice. I hope you look kindly on me for it.

We spoke about God recently, and I want to explain that further. I will wait until the end before I share my purpose in full, but discussing God won't ruin anything.

I believe in him, and if we had more time together, I'm sure I could prove his existence to you.

I believe in God, and I hate him.

He may be the only creature that I feel such a strong emotion toward. You told me that I've never cared for anyone, but that's not true. I used to care deeply, but it was God who showed me how foolish such notions were. Soon, depending on your choice, you'll begin to research me as you do the criminals you chase.

It's going to be hard for you to discover the truth about my past. I've gone to great lengths to distort portions of it and completely change others. Your mind may be able to overcome some of my deceit, though I doubt all of it.

The official record shows that I was born in Los Angeles, but that's false.

My mother birthed me in a small, west Mexican town. The kind you see in movies, where there's one bank, one major road, and no subdivisions. The major road held all the businesses, and the back roads the houses. None of them were nearly as nice as the one I currently occupy. Its one-story layout was done purposefully to remind me of my past.

I've hidden my past from the world, but not because I'm ashamed. I'm proud of my past. It made me into who I am today.

Without it, I would have accomplished nothing.

I had a brother. His name was Mark. My mother had a penchant for biblical names. She wasn't an educated woman, and she bore two children out of wedlock.

I'm wondering how much to tell you. It isn't fear that keeps me from revealing everything, only hesitation because you're the first person I have shared this with. You should consider it a great honor. I've met no one else in life that I would even consider showing my world to.

I do it partly out of respect and partly to thank you. Your mind is a wonder, even to me, and how you've harnessed it to do your bidding is something to be commended. To be admired, even. Well done.

I want to thank you because you've made this possible. Your naiveté and strong desire to make the world a better place. It's unfortunate that your desires are in such stark contrast with mine.

Let this letter be that then, my sincere appreciation for everything you've done.

The next will be about my past. About my mother and brother and how God set me on this quest.

Yours,

Luke Titan, MD, Ph.D., Special Agent for the Federal Bureau of Investigations

CHAPTER SIXTEEN

In the end, Luke decided the best route was the most direct. He couldn't waste time trying to talk to Christian or slinking around when he thought Christian was busy. He needed to know what the boy was thinking *now*.

Christian went to bed at three in the morning. He was sleeping less than Luke, which was a good thing. Sleep deprivation slowed down people's minds and made them more susceptible to suggestion. It also meant that when they *did* sleep, they slept deeply, their body trying to make up for lost time.

Luke waited until Christian fell asleep, then went to his car. He drove east through Atlanta's streets. It took him thirty minutes, which was what he wanted. Just enough time for Christian to drop into a deep sleep.

He parked the car at Christian's curb and stepped out.

In a heroic act for Christian, a year or so ago, he had given both Luke and Tommy keys to his house in case they ever needed to get inside. Luke used the key to gain entry.

A rapid beeping sounded from the alarm system, and Luke punched in the code that he had watched Christian use many times, shutting it off.

He walked through the house without any noise revealing his presence. Christian's bedroom door was open.

Luke entered, stepping just inside. Christian was on his side with his legs curled up near his torso. His breathing was even, and the soft moonlight shining in showed Luke that the boy's eyes were still. He wasn't dreaming yet. Perhaps Luke's presence would give him something to dream about, even if only his subconscious knew it.

Luke went to the nightstand where Christian had left his laptop. He looked at Christian for another second. The moonlight made his face look even more haggard than usual.

It'll be over soon, Luke thought.

He took the laptop to the living room and sat on the couch. He opened the laptop and punched in another password. Christian had created a new one last year, and Luke found it obnoxiously adorable. The new one, of course, was *VeronicaLopez.*

Christian wasn't worried about being hacked. His naiveté coming into play again.

Luke pulled a USB drive from his pocket and plugged it into the computer's port. It only took a few seconds to load the program. He paused, listening for any movement in the house.

Everything was still.

He spent the next half-hour finding everything he

could before closing the computer. The rest was waiting for him at home, including any future work Christian did.

Luke left the house, not liking what he'd seen one bit.

Chanice had been doing well. She had been playing along just as Sarah had asked her to. Two or three nights had passed, and Chanice had remained quiet. She'd even let Ted talk to her. Sarah had been feeling hopeful the other woman had turned a corner and would survive.

Until tonight.

Ted was sitting Indian-style in front of Chanice, but he'd gotten too close. She lashed out, her thin black arm like a supersonic boomerang.

Ted screamed like a girl who'd just felt a bee buzz by her face. His hand went to his cheek where Chanice's nails had cut four scratches horizontally across his face.

The blood was dark, a stream from each line running down his skin like oil.

Ted pulled his hand away and looked at the blood, his eyes wide as if he'd never seen the substance before. Or, at least, not his own. He looked back at Chanice.

Goddammit, she was smiling. Her hand flashed again, catching the other side of Ted's face.

He screamed and scooted away, pushing his ass back across the floor. He stared for a second, clearly unable to believe she'd hurt him. Streaks of blood ran down both sides of his face, growing thicker with each passing second.

"Yeah, you white motherfucker. Come get some more,"

Chanice snarled. Rage rippled in each word like wind against a kite.

Ted turned to Sarah, and the disbelief written across his bloody face was comical. As if he didn't understand why one of his wives had *hurt* him.

Then his face changed, and whatever comedy Sarah had found at the moment disappeared like smoke in a heavy wind. He ignored Chanice and turned to stare accusingly at Sarah.

His wide eyes shrunk to slits and his lips, which had been pulled back in fear, turned into thin lines below his nose. He didn't need to say anything, not in the basement shadows with blood running down his face. His expression said enough.

You did this, Sarah. I trusted you to make sure I didn't need to hurt anyone. But now I do. It's your fault.

Sarah heard the words as clearly as if Ted had spoken them aloud. Maybe he did. Maybe Sarah couldn't tell the difference between reality and her imagination anymore.

It didn't matter because Ted stood and walked to the basement's corner.

Sarah screamed, *"Please! Please, no!"* Tears rushed to her eyes. She didn't hear what Chanice said next. She was too focused on what was coming.

Ted walked into the light again. The mallet was in his right hand, and Sarah saw Keely's hair on it. Two strands, looking blonde in the awful yellow light stemming from above the stairs.

He didn't clean it, Sarah thought. *He didn't clean the mallet. He's going to hit Chanice with it, and the hair will mix. The hair will mix!*

"The hair will mix!" she screamed, not realizing what she was thinking or saying.

Ted looked at her with his head cocked slightly to the side. He stared for a second but focused on Chanice when she screamed at him.

"Come on, you poor white fuck. I'd rather die than sit here and listen to any more of your shit!"

Ted moved more carefully than he had when he'd approached Keely. Chanice was on her feet, her arms raised from her sides and her palms out facing Ted. She looked almost like Catwoman, ready to pounce, except for the chains connecting her to the wall.

"No, no, no, no," Sarah repeated over and over, unable to stop, yet not aware she was speaking.

Ted stood with the mallet hanging loose by his waist.

"I'll wait." He half-turned as if he was going to leave.

Sarah felt a brief sense of hope rising in her. She would be saved from having gotten Chanice killed.

Ted turned back faster than Sarah believed he could, his hand raising the mallet in a crazy backswing. Chanice's eyes widened and she froze in place, too shocked to duck. The mallet whipped through the air and collided with her jaw.

Sarah moaned as Chanice's face stretched and her bones crunched.

Chanice let out an animalistic scream, sounding like a small creature caught in a trap. Her hands went to her mouth.

Ted swung the mallet again, this time from over his head. The mallet connected directly with Chanice's nose, splitting her face like an overripe avocado.

The mallet came down again. Right on top of Chanice's head. A stream of blood flowed from the corner of her right eye as she collapsed to the floor, her dead stare looking out across the concrete.

Ted turned to Sarah, but she only stared at the dead woman on the floor.

"I asked you, very nicely, to make sure she remained civil. You did this. Not me. This is *your* fault."

The problem, as Luke saw it, was that Christian had stopped caring. It was obvious from his computer that he planned on leaving the FBI once he'd finished with Ted Hinson. He planned to walk into Ted's house, find the women, and kill Hinson.

Christian was okay with doing jail time if necessary.

Luke had to stop it from taking place. Not the jail time, but Christian killing Hinson just yet. He walked into Tommy's office and shut the door behind him.

Tommy covered the phone held to his ear and looked at Luke questioningly.

Luke motioned for him to hang up.

"Hey, something just came up that's pretty important. Can I call you back in a few minutes? Sure. Thanks." He put the phone down. "I hope this *is* important. That was the cop who found the body yesterday."

"It's Christian," Luke said. "I think he's about to do something very foolish."

"What do you mean?"

Luke walked to Tommy's desk. "He's going after Hinson."

"How do you know?"

"He told me, in so many words."

"What? When?" Tommy asked.

"Last night. He showed up late like he used to."

"What exactly did he say?"

"That he couldn't stand by while people were being kidnapped. Not even if Waverly ordered him to drop it."

"Jesus Christ," Tommy said. "What did you tell him?"

"That he needed to calm down."

The two men stared at each other for a moment.

"Is he here today?" Tommy asked.

"Yes," Luke said. "In his office."

"Well, let's go down there." Tommy got to his feet.

"Think that through. What will happen if we confront him? He'll say he has no such plans, and he'll stop telling me whatever he *is* thinking."

Tommy sat back down. "So what do we do?"

"First, you can't tell him I told you this, okay?"

"Why?" Tommy asked.

"Because it violates trust he put in me. If he asks, just say you figured it out."

"Fine. It won't matter if the kid kills someone. What are we going to do?"

"We have to follow him," Luke said. "We have to catch him in the act, right before he makes his move."

"Put a tail on Christian? That's what you're suggesting?"

Luke nodded, his face solemn. "But not anyone else. You and me. I don't want to get him in trouble, which is what will happen if we put someone else on him. We'll take turns watching. I don't think it will take long."

Tommy shook his head and looked at his desk. "Alice… She'll understand, I suppose." He sighed. "You're sure about this?"

"I wouldn't bring it to you if I wasn't."

"Goddammit. Aren't either of the two shrinks he's seeing helping him at all? He's losing his mind. He is."

"When we catch him in the act, we give him an ultimatum. Either he sincerely gets help and willingly steps aside for a few months, or we go to Waverly."

Tommy sighed. "Okay. How do we do it? Each of us takes a night shift and switch off every other night? What if he doesn't show up to work again?"

"Yes, that's how the nights should work. I'll take the first shift. If he doesn't show up to work, we'll know from whoever is on him the previous night. We don't come off our shift until we know he's arrived here."

"So we'll do twenty-four hours on, eight off, indefinitely?"

"Trust me," Luke said. "It won't last long."

Veronica lay on the couch with Christian. He wasn't ready to come to her place yet, but he had let her come to his house again.

Still, she was here, and so was he, and that was what mattered.

Veronica had her head in his lap while they sat on the couch. The television was on one of her guilty pleasure shows, *The Real Housewives of Atlanta.* She knew Christian couldn't stand it, but he put up with it.

She secretly thought he didn't watch. He fell into his thoughts and was fine there. His mind did things that she'd never be able to understand.

"Veronica?" he said.

"Yeah."

"I need to ask you something."

She sat up and pressed pause on the remote. The show stopped playing, and she turned so she faced him.

"We're not back together. Are we?" he asked, sounding almost like a child.

Christian used to get like this sometimes, especially when discussing anything to do with their relationship. He was like a kid in a dinosaur museum, asking questions about things he didn't understand.

"No. We're hanging out."

"But you want to be with me?"

A simple question, but one with a very complex answer. Veronica understood he couldn't handle the complexity. Not when it came to *them.* The man's mind could do acrobatic feats with numbers and people's motives, but when it came to his personal relationships, he needed simplicity.

"I want you to be healthy, Christian. When you are, I'd like to try again, yes."

"I want to be healthy, too," he said. "I think I know how to be. Or rather, how to get there."

"How?"

"I don't want to talk about that yet. I wanted to ask you something about the future."

"Shoot," she said.

"If I had to leave for a few years, do you think you'd wait? If you knew when I returned that I'd be with you. If the reason I left was so I *could* be healthy?"

Veronica was quiet for a few moments. "I don't know," she whispered. "Years are a long time."

He nodded and said nothing.

"Where would you go?"

"Let's watch TV. I don't want to talk about it yet. I just wanted to see what you'd say."

Veronica kept looking at him, but he remained fixed on the television. "You sure?"

He nodded. Veronica lay back down, putting her head on his lap again. She hit play, but she found it hard to focus. She didn't like how Christian sounded when he asked that question. Why would he have to go away? Where would he go? A clinic? An asylum?

There were too many questions, and Christian wouldn't answer any of them.

Luke passed the night in a rental Toyota Corolla, silence reigning. He never needed much sleep, a few hours a night at most. These next few nights would be simple.

He was annoyed that he'd had to rent a vehicle for this stakeout, but he couldn't use his Tesla. Christian would spot it if he looked outside. An FBI sedan wouldn't work either. Christian would also have questions if he saw one of those.

Luke had been concerned that Christian might attempt killing Hinson too soon, or he had been until Veronica showed up. Christian wouldn't leave the house tonight. That was good, but Luke needed four days. Christian had to hold off that long if his plan was to work.

Four days, Christian. That's all I need of you, and you'll be free of me forever.

CHAPTER SEVENTEEN

Christian put his slippers on and stared down at them, thinking about his conversation with Veronica the previous night. It had confirmed the decision he had made.

Maybe she wouldn't wait for him, but she was right. He needed to be healthy. He had called his mother from work today and told her that he wanted to go back to the person he used to be. She'd cried into the phone, and his heart had broken, knowing what he'd done to her over the past year.

Christian had left work on time today and gone home. He'd cooked himself dinner for the first time in ages, although "cook" was a strong term for the four peanut butter and jelly sandwiches he'd made. It was the most he'd eaten at once in a while.

After eating, he'd called his mother again and actually *talked* to her. He'd listened to what she had done in the past week, and was careful to avoid giving her too much detail about himself. He didn't want her worrying.

Christian needed to speak with someone else, but he'd waited for tonight to do it.

He pulled his phone out and loaded the Uber app.

This was the second night of the stakeout, and Tommy's turn for duty. He pulled away from the curb and started following Christian's ride.

Tommy didn't believe that Christian would take an Uber to Ted Hinson's home. When the Uber pulled onto the highway, he recognized that they weren't heading toward Hinson's neighborhood, which was a relief, although Tommy still didn't know where they were going.

The coffee sitting in his cup holder was cold and nearly empty. He reached into his glove compartment, keeping one hand on the wheel, and pulled out a bottle of caffeine pills. He dry swallowed one, then tossed the bottle onto the passenger seat.

Christian had acted almost normally today. He was quieter than usual, but other than that, the gloom that usually followed him around like a storm cloud seemed to have lifted. Maybe Luke's assessment was wrong and the kid was turning a corner and coming back to the land of the living.

Tommy grabbed his cellphone from the passenger seat. "Siri, call Luke Titan," he said to the digital assistant programmed into it.

"Is he moving?" Luke answered, sounding as if sleep wasn't calling on him nearly as hard as it was Tommy.

He would never understand either of his partners. Not their minds nor their strange patterns—including Luke's sleep schedule. "Yeah, he is. I think he's coming to your house. Has he called you?"

"No, but he wouldn't. He stopped calling before arriving a long time ago."

"Well, unless he has a side chick in your part of town, he's on his way to you. I don't see Christian having a bunch of women waiting on him to come over, though."

"Okay," he said. "You're going to stay on my street, right?"

"Yeah, I'll wait until he leaves, then keep following."

"Good."

"Later." Tommy hung up the phone. He let his car fall back another hundred feet, hoping the caffeine would kick in soon.

Luke understood what Christian was doing. Tying up loose ends and trying to mend relationships was classic behavior for someone who didn't see a way out of their situation.

Christian's conversation with Veronica had been endearing, perhaps even noble. Now, he was coming to Luke's house to do something similar.

Luke watched the Uber's lights turn into the driveway. Christian stepped out of the car, handed the driver a tip through the open window, and padded in his slippers to Luke's front door.

At least he had worn shoes this time, usually he showed up barefoot.

The doorbell rang and Luke waited a few moments

before standing up from his chair. On the second ring, he opened the door.

"Having a tough time sleeping?" Luke asked.

"Can I come in?"

"Rare that you ask. Sure." He moved back to let Christian walk through the doorway.

Christian paused once inside, another rarity, and turned to Luke as he shut the door. "I don't think I ever asked where you'd like to talk. I normally just head to the living room. You want to talk in there, or somewhere else?"

Luke smiled. "You're behaving strangely."

"I'm feeling a bit strange."

"If it's my choice, let's go to the kitchen. I'll make some coffee."

Luke led the way and Christian followed. Luke went to the counter and put a Keurig cup in the machine. "I assume you don't want any?"

"Actually, I'll take some."

Without turning around, Luke said, "You *are* acting strange."

He made the two cups in silence and handed one to Christian when finished. "What brings you over?"

Christian took the cup and held it like it was a foreign object. "You remember what we talked about the other night?"

Luke nodded. "Faith. In God. In you."

"Have you thought any more about Hinson? Looked into him at all?"

"No."

A pause ensued. "Don't you want to ask me the same question?" Christian asked.

Luke shook his head. "There's no need. I doubt you've been thinking of much else."

Christian smiled awkwardly, probably because he rarely did it anymore. "I've been thinking of other things lately. I guess, the other night, you sort of gave me permission to do what I need. Just like you gave me permission to do what was needed with Speckle."

"Is that what I did?"

"Yes, in a way. I hated you for it for a long time. I don't know if I ever admitted that to myself." Christian pulled his cigarettes out, paying no attention to himself. He went so far as to put one in his mouth before realizing what he was doing. "Shit, I'm sorry. Do you mind if we go outside so I can smoke this?"

"Not at all," Luke said.

The two walked through his kitchen to the backyard. It was even larger than the front, with a patio that Luke had created with kings in mind.

They sat beneath the canopy that covered the whole area. Overstuffed pillows filled both of the wicker couches, and a stone table sat between them.

Christian lit his cigarette, and Luke waited for him to continue talking.

"I hated you for making me do that. Or at least, I thought I did. Now, I think you gave me permission to be what was needed at the time. We wouldn't have made it out alive, otherwise. None of us." Christian met Luke's eyes. His cigarette's red glow was mirrored in them. "The other night, you did it again. Did you know you were? Don't lie to me."

"I don't lie to you, Christian. I had some inclination that you needed to hear what I was saying."

"Do you still believe it?"

Luke nodded.

"Let me hear you say it."

"I still believe it."

"So do I. I guess I came over here tonight to tell you that. I'm going to stop Hinson, and I hope you don't try to stop me." He looked down at his slippers. "I don't think you will, though. You know I need to do this if I'm ever going to have a chance at a real life again. I suppose you also know that I'll be done at the FBI."

Luke nodded.

"I'll never be as good of a host as you," Christian said as he looked at the cigarettes on his lap. "Would you like one?"

"Sure."

"Not worried about cancer?" Christian said, smiling as he pulled out two more cigarettes. He handed one and his lighter across to Luke.

"I don't worry, Christian."

"I know. Where do you want me to put this?" he said, holding his finished cigarette.

"Here." Luke reached over the table at the end of the couch and handed Christian an ashtray, then lit his cigarette and passed back the lighter.

"You won't tell Tommy?"

"No," Luke said. "Not until the time is right."

"Good." Christian nodded. "I'm going to talk to him, too, but it'll probably be after everything happens. Out of everyone involved, he's the one who is still a boy scout. He won't understand."

"You're sure Hinson is guilty? Absolutely?"

"I'm sure. Those women are still there, I think. If not, there'll be evidence of murder."

"Have you gone to your mansion?" Luke asked. "Has it shown you anything?"

"Not in a while. I don't need to for this."

Luke nodded and the two of them smoked in silence. Once finished, Luke walked his partner to the door and saw him off.

Two more days, Christian. Please give me those, he thought as he closed the door.

CHAPTER EIGHTEEN

Two days passed for Christian. They were the best two days he could remember having in a long, long time. His mind was at peace.

The day after he saw Luke, he went over to Veronica's house and spent the night. She'd tried to bring up what he had mentioned earlier in the week, but he'd told her he wasn't ready to discuss it yet.

Christian didn't know exactly what would happen at Hinson's house, so he wouldn't talk about the future. If he could subdue Hinson, then he would lose his badge but he wouldn't see jail time.

He knew Hinson's outcome wouldn't end in jail time since the arrest wouldn't be constitutionally legal, but Hinson wouldn't be able to kidnap women ever again. He'd be on a watch list for the rest of his life.

If Christian couldn't arrest him, then he'd kill him. He held no doubt about his ability or desire to do so.

Yes, he'd kill Ted Hinson if need be. Perhaps even if it

wasn't needed. He hadn't decided on that yet. If Hinson died, then Christian would face some jail time. Probably not a lot. Given his service record, and the evidence that would be found at Hinson's house, he might even get off with parole.

The possibility of prison existed, though, and Christian would explain everything to Veronica when Hinson was finished.

One way or another.

Christian had waited until Thursday night to head to Hinson's house. If Hinson planned on leaving for another weekend getaway, wanting another souvenir, he'd leave on Friday. Christian's best chance of finding Hinson at home was tonight.

He put on his tennis shoes and tied the laces tight. The shoes went with his short sleeve shirt and a pair of sweatpants. He placed his holster across his body, and over it all, a long jacket.

He'd checked out an FBI cruiser this afternoon and drove it home. Uber wouldn't work tonight, unfortunately.

Christian smiled at the thought of saving some money.

His mind was a crazy place, whether sane or insane. He'd never be able to stop some of the weird things he came up with.

Fully dressed and ready to end all of this, he walked out into the night. He didn't even bother locking his door as he left.

Happiness, perhaps the purest he'd ever felt, abounded.

"Here we go," Tommy said to himself. He was no longer tired and hadn't been since he'd watched Christian pull out of the FBI parking lot in one of their vehicles. He had called Luke.

"Tonight's the night."

"How do you know?" Luke had asked.

"He checked out a car."

"You okay out there alone tonight? I finally need a few hours of sleep, I think."

"Yeah. I'll just follow him to the house and stop him before he goes in. He won't draw his weapon on me, and the kid can't physically take me if I have to bring him down."

"Call me if you need backup. I'll wake up."

"I'll call you when it's over," Tommy had answered.

If Luke said he needed sleep, then the man really needed it. Tommy didn't think having Luke there would matter much, except maybe when it came to talking some sense into Christian. He listened to Luke in a way that he didn't listen to others, but that was because of Luke's brainpower. Tommy could handle the interception by himself.

He was wired, adrenaline coursing through his veins as he followed Christian's car. Tommy had programmed in Ted Hinson's house into his GPS, and sure enough, Christian was following the same roads.

Tommy didn't understand how things had gone so far down this path, to the point that he would have to prevent his partner from murdering someone. He didn't feel guilty for not alerting the FBI. Christian was family, and if family veered from the correct course, you brought them back. You didn't ask other people to do it.

Once he had Christian in his custody, he'd ensure the correct actions were taken. Either Christian got serious help, or he left the FBI. Tommy would hate to see him go, but he also didn't think this place was right for Christian.

It took a certain type of mind to function in this environment, one that could view humans as something different when they were on the other side of the line. Tommy had learned a long time ago that he wasn't chasing people, but felons. He saw them as a different species, and that belief allowed him to sleep at night.

Christian couldn't do that. People would always be people to him, and with his brain's horsepower, that created a dangerous psychological problem.

An hour passed as they both drove toward Athens.

Finally, they reached Hinson's neighborhood, and Tommy's introspection ended. An alert calm came over him, his senses and training dominating his persona.

Tommy had kept his distance from Christian's car during the drive, staying far enough back to see his taillights but little else. He sped up as Christian turned into the neighborhood, flooring it to over seventy. He slowed as he approached where Christian had turned, then whipped the vehicle right.

Christian's car was parked by the curb.

Tommy sped up, needing to stop the kid before he reached Hinson's door. His tires squealed as he threw his car into park across the street from Christian's car. Christian looked over his car roof as Tommy stepped onto the street.

"Get in my car, Christian."

The kid cocked his head to the side as if he didn't understand what was happening.

"Get the fuck in," Tommy said.

"No."

Christian started walking up the street without looking back to see what his partner did.

Tommy jogged to the other side of the street and got ahead of Christian, stopping him from moving forward. "You're not going in there, Christian. You need to understand that right now, before anything else. Whatever you wanted to do, it's over."

Neither Tommy nor Christian reached for their weapons, although Tommy was fully aware of Christian's hands.

"I'm going in," Christian said. "It's the only way to stop all this. Everything going on in my head. It's the only way to make sure Hinson stops what he's doing. Get out of my way, Tommy."

"Listen to me. It's over. You know there's nothing you can do besides kill me, and we both know you don't want to hurt me. I'm not letting you go into that house. Don't make me take you down."

Tommy saw a raw determination in Christian that Luke never displayed, despite their similar minds. Luke was always calm, always in control. But when Christian's mind took off, nothing stopped it.

He stepped around Tommy.

Tommy didn't hesitate. He wrapped his right arm around Christian's neck and hooked it to his left arm.

It only took about fifteen seconds for Christian to lose consciousness.

***

Ted had lost control. He knew that now. It always took him a few days to come to his senses and realize the mistakes he had made when his anger took over.

He had called in sick to work for the entire week. He couldn't go in with scratches across each side of his face. He was healing quickly, but thought he might have to call out next week, too. The scratches would raise questions Ted couldn't answer.

He was also concerned with the basement.

He had been rash. Far too rash.

His mind kept returning to what he had done, wanting him to stare at his mistakes in reality's cold light.

Only flashes of what he'd done came to him this time, and that's how he knew he'd gone overboard.

He remembered the mallet. The feel of it in his hand, the weight of the thing.

He remembered screaming at Sarah, *"You did this! You! You! You!"*

Ted hadn't been looking at the person he'd been screaming at. He had been looking at the other three women he had taken the mallet to.

He hadn't even remembered his wives' names in the moment. Everything was ruined because he'd had to kill another one, and he'd gone on to kill three more by bashing their heads in with the rubber mallet.

Two women remained alive in his basement. Sarah and Julie. The four dead bodies were still down there with them. Ted hadn't even started thinking about how he'd clean everything up. Keely had been easy. One body could be disposed of easily, but four?

He didn't know how, and that led him to his next decision. He thought that he might be losing his mind, but shoved that thought aside. Hinsons didn't lose their minds. Poor people did that. They were the crazies you saw at traffic lights, hustling for money.

Ted wasn't losing his mind. He was getting his family back.

He was done worrying about getting other women to love him. He decided he would kill Sarah and Julie as soon as Christy and Callie were back under his roof.

Or maybe he would just move into Christy's house if she preferred staying there. That could work. He would then come back here and kill the two women, then slowly get rid of the bodies.

It had been silly, the whole thing. Trying to recreate a family when his lived right across town. Christy would just have to see it his way. They were far better together than apart.

It was nearing one in the morning on Thursday night when Ted left his house. He was going to get his wife back, just like the heroes in romances did.

Tommy kept to his word and didn't call when Christian finally left his house.

Luke had stood beneath a tree's shadow in Christian's neighborhood and watched Tommy and Christian drive off into the night.

Luke knew it would take an hour to get to Athens from Atlanta, which constrained his timeline. Everyone had to work with what the world gave them, however.

He had parked the rental car the next neighborhood over. Tommy was a good detective, and even a poor one would have noticed if he'd been in his own car. Luke ran back to his car, his lungs and legs easily carrying him the tenth of a mile through backyards.

He started the engine and pulled onto the road much faster than Christian or Tommy had. It took him ten minutes to reach his destination.

Luke parked his car in Tommy's spot and donned the ski mask. He moved quickly through the parking deck. Tommy's building had cameras, but security wasn't tight. One man sat at a desk in the lobby, and Luke wasn't going anywhere near him.

He used the key Tommy had made for everyone at Christian's insistence and took the residents' elevator to the correct floor.

It was late, but not *that* late. People might still be moving around, and if so, Luke was prepared to kill them.

Luck, as it so often seemed to be, was on his side tonight. Luke used the key to open the door, then he took off the mask and placed it in his back pocket. He hated to operate this quickly, but for once he couldn't dictate the speed of things. He was at Tommy's and Christian's mercy.

He heard the television in the living room. The voices

stopped, meaning that Tommy's fiancée had heard the door open.

"Tommy?" she called.

"It's Luke, Alice. Tommy asked me to come over. Something has happened with Christian."

He closed the door as Alice's footfalls came to meet him.

"What happened?" She halted as she turned the corner, shock and fear straining her face.

A woman's intuition existed. While Luke wasn't masking his face, a man in a similar situation would have continued talking.

Alice didn't. She saw only one thing in Luke's face. Murder.

Intuition wouldn't save Alice, however. She took off. Unable to run to the front door, she headed to the back bedroom with the intent to lock Luke out and call for help.

Luke moved with lethal precision, catching her before she reached the end of the living room. In a mirror of the move that Tommy would use shortly in another part of Georgia, he wrapped his arms around her neck until unconsciousness overtook her.

Luke let her collapse to the floor. There was no time for inaction. He put the mask back on, and with an ease that belied his frame, threw her over his shoulder. He pulled his pistol out from the back of his pants.

If anyone saw him carrying Alice out, their lives would end like so many others who had come into contact with the real Luke Titan.

There was one more thing to do, and this would cause the most noise out of the whole endeavor. Luke closed the door behind him, using the key to lock it once he was outside.

Then he turned and launched his foot at the door. The kick landed true, and the door frame shattered.

The door banged back against the wall, but Luke was already leaving the building.

MARRIAGE

CHAPTER NINETEEN

Christian woke up slumped down in the seat on the passenger side of Tommy's car. He blinked a few times before looking around. He remembered everything until the moment he went under.

"Where are we?" Christian whispered as he pulled himself up.

"Outside my place."

Christian looked through the window and saw Tommy's building. "Why did you stop me?"

"You know why."

"Luke told you?"

"It doesn't matter, Christian. You can't do what you were planning."

"It matters to me. Did Luke tell you?"

"No," Tommy said. "It wasn't hard to figure out on my own."

"Does Luke know you have me?"

"Yes. I called him after I put you in the car."

"What did he say?" Christian asked.

"He's on his way over."

Christian said nothing and the two sat in silence until Luke's Tesla pulled up.

He wouldn't mention any of their conversations. Luke had kept his word about not telling anyone. Whatever came next, Christian wouldn't bring him down, even as he fell himself.

This was his fault. He hadn't paid enough attention and hadn't realized Tommy was figuring everything out on his own. He certainly didn't have any idea that he was being followed.

"Let's go upstairs," Tommy said when Luke got out of his car and came over to them.

"Is Alice here?" Christian didn't want anyone else knowing about this. He had an idea of what would happen next, and he didn't need the embarrassment of someone else watching it all transpire.

"She's asleep. We'll go to my office to talk."

The office would work, Christian supposed. It was on the other side of the condominium.

No one said anything as they went through the main entrance.

Two police officers stood next to the security guard. Both had been leaning against the guard's desk, but now they turned to the three FBI agents.

"Mr. Phillips," the security guard said as they entered the lobby. "We've been trying to reach you for the past hour."

"My phone's off. I was working."

"Agent Phillips, I'm Officer Vidak and this is Officer Alain. We need to speak with you immediately."

"What's going on?" Tommy said.

Luke and Christian stepped up to flank their partner. Christian did it subconsciously. He didn't notice Luke doing the same. Whatever had happened between him and Tommy, it wasn't important right now. Protection of their own was all that mattered.

"We'd like to talk in the manager's office," Vidak said.

"Why not in my condo?" Tommy asked.

"There are officers working up there right now."

"Where's Alice?" Tommy said. The obvious question, because if she wasn't down here with these cops, and they didn't want anyone going upstairs, then where the hell was she?

"Come with us, please, sir," Vidak said.

"Where the fuck is Alice?" Tommy's voice had been calm when speaking to Christian, a technique that he'd seen his partner use when talking to perps. Now, his calm had been erased, replaced with heat burning from a furnace of fear deep inside his chest.

"She's missing, Agent Phillips. That's why we need to speak."

Tommy ran straight past the cops, leaving Luke and Christian behind. He rounded the corner but everyone knew he was headed upstairs.

"Let's go," Alain said.

The four of them hustled across the lobby, leaving the security guard staring slack jawed after them. They reached the elevator but Tommy was already gone. They pressed the call button and waited.

"What happened?" Luke said.

"There was a break in. Ms. Stromin is gone. There doesn't appear to be anything else taken."

Luke and Christian looked at each other for a second, knowledge passing between them as surely as if they were telepathic.

Ted Hinson. It's him.

They entered the elevator and followed Tommy to his floor.

"Alice!" Tommy screamed as he stormed into the condo. His mind barely registered the broken door. He moved through the house as agile as an eighteen-year-old athlete, ignoring the officers all around his home. He stopped in the bedroom, the final room of the house. She wasn't *here*.

"Tommy," Luke called.

Tommy turned.

"This isn't what you want to hear right now, but you need to talk to the police."

"We'll find her," Christian said. "We'll find her."

Tommy looked at the two of them, feeling tears threatening to overwhelm him. He couldn't cry right now, and he knew it. He had to focus because his fiancée was missing.

Another case, he thought. *Another fucking case. Cold and detached. That's what Alice needs right now. Not you sobbing in front of cops who are trying to find her.*

In that moment, his mind came as close as it ever would to resembling Christian's. His shoulders straightened and his hands stopped shaking. The tears threatening to pour from his eyes disappeared, his mind listening to his commands like a computer system.

He walked past Luke and Christian, heading to the living room.

"Who's in charge?" he asked the cops.

"I am," Vidak said.

Tommy nodded with grim determination. "Let's talk."

The sun was just coming up over the horizon and people were beginning to fill the FBI building. Neither Christian nor Luke had slept, and Tommy was still at the police station answering questions.

"Let's give it a shot," Christian said.

Luke nodded and hit the speakerphone on his desk to dial Waverly's cell. Very few agents in the bureau had the number, and none of them had ever used it. Now was the time, if there had ever been one.

"Hello?" the FBI director answered.

"Sir, it's Luke Titan. I'm here with Christian Windsor."

A pause on the line, then Waverly responded, "I'm guessing this is important."

"Yes, sir," Christian said. "It couldn't wait to go through your assistant."

"I'm listening."

Christian could tell Waverly was still pissed from their last interaction. It didn't matter, though. That would all disappear momentarily.

"There was a break-in at Tommy's apartment last

night," Luke said. "His fiancée, Alice Stromin, was kidnapped."

A longer silence ensued. Christian looked up at Luke, his face indecipherable.

"What do we know?" the director finally asked.

"Not much yet," Luke said. "Nothing else in the condominium was disturbed. The door was kicked in, which means she probably didn't know the intruder. Neighbors called the police when they heard the door, but the intruder was gone before anyone arrived."

"I'm going to regret this question. I already know it. Do you think this has anything to do with Hinson? Before you answer, remember that in my mind he is one hundred percent innocent. So *think* before you respond."

Christian wasn't going to say a word. Anything from him on the subject would be discarded as fanciful delusions.

"Sir, we think it's a possibility," Luke said.

"What do you need?" Waverly asked.

"Twenty-four hour surveillance on Hinson," Luke continued. "A warrant to search his house would be preferable."

"Surveillance is a go. The warrant will take some time, if it's even possible, especially after the bullshit you two pulled. What else do you need?"

"Is a warrant for his internet history possible?" Christian asked.

"Maybe, but doubtful. Again, consider your answers carefully before speaking. What do you think this man is doing with the women?"

Christian and Luke looked at each other. Christian

didn't know because he hadn't spent any time in his mansion learning about Hinson. His purpose had been singular. Stop him, without trying to understand anything.

"We don't know, sir," Luke said.

"Windsor, you don't have any idea? That big brain of yours didn't come up with some theories?"

"I dropped the case, sir," Christian said.

A brief pause.

"Why would he take Tommy's fiancée?" Waverly asked.

"Sir, pardon my language, but we think it might be a 'fuck you' to us," Luke said.

"If that's true, he's going to regret taking his first breath on this world. Do you have any other idea who might have done this? Where's Tommy?"

"He's at the police precinct answering questions," Christian said.

"Does he have any idea who else this could be?"

"No, sir. He didn't even mention Hinson."

Silence again.

"Okay, this is what's going to happen. I want a team of twelve on this from our side. Six people in pairs working eight hour shifts on Hinson. The other six working with the police to chase any and all possible leads. Luke, you're running point. I'll have my assistant email you the list of people working with you on this, and if you need more resources, you tell me. I want this on national and local news by the end of the morning. I'll handle that part. We have two days to find this woman and we're going to do it by the book. Have Tommy call me on my cell the moment you see him. Call me at noon and let me know where we're at. Anything else right now?"

"We should speak with his ex-wife, sir," Luke said.

"Okay, we can add more men to protect her if necessary."

"Sir, I'd like to stop by there first," Luke said.

"Why?" Waverly asked.

Luke looked at Christian, a glint in his eyes. "He knows me. If they're close, and I show up there, it'll send a message."

Waverly was quiet for a second, and Christian knew he was thinking it over. "Okay, fine. Let's talk at noon."

The line went dead.

Christian leaned back in his chair, his shoulders relaxing from the tension they'd held through the entire conversation. A supreme feeling of gratitude washed over him.

All the anger and hate he'd felt toward Waverly over what happened in DC dissipated. The director had acted decisively and forcefully, trusting his two agents and assigning resources to look for other possibilities. He'd acted correctly.

Christian now understood why he was in that position. Waverly would never be found in front of a suspected murderer's house, prepared to kill him without writ or warrant. But when it counted, he *acted*.

"We need to go to the precinct," Luke said.

"Yeah." Christian stood and the two left the office.

Tommy was still in Vadik's office. Officer Alain was in a chair a few feet away with a notepad in front of him. He had been here for hours, although he'd lost count of how long a while ago. Time only mattered in that each second gone meant Alice was still missing.

Luke tapped on the office's glass door and Vadik waved him and Christian in.

"Hey," Vadik said, both he and Alain standing as the two entered.

"Hello," Luke said. Christian was quiet.

The two moved to either side of Tommy, though he didn't stand. He felt Luke's hand rest on his shoulder.

"The director wants you to call him as soon as you're done here," Luke said.

Tommy looked up. "You called him?"

Christian smiled, looking like a teenager who just played a prank. "On his cell. At five in the morning."

"We're going all in," Luke said. "We got the email just before we arrived here. Twelve agents are being trans-ferred to us, which is partly why we came."

"Hold on, if you don't mind," Vadik said. "The director? Who are we talking about?"

"The FBI director," Luke said. "Alan Waverly."

Both police officers sat, but neither said anything.

"Look," Tommy said. "There isn't going to be any juris-dictional shit on this. We're working together to find her. That's it. Okay?"

"Yeah, yeah, of course," Vadik said.

"Sure," Alain agreed.

"We're giving six of those agents to you," Luke said. "They'll have all the resources of the FBI at their disposal. I mean that literally. I don't want to tell you two gentlemen how to do your jobs, and I'm sure I don't need to, but their directives are to follow every possible lead. The director's given us two days to find Alice, and he means to have her back by then."

Tommy felt tears threatening again for the first time since he'd stood in his bedroom. He didn't know the exact emotion, maybe thankfulness, maybe sadness, maybe happiness. He couldn't tell. He only knew the cavalry was coming.

"When will they be here?" Vadik said.

"All twelve are from the Atlanta office. The six coming to you will be here within the hour."

Vadik looked at his watch, then glanced at Alain. "Okay."

Tommy read the look of fear, dread, and excitement all mixed together. He imagined they were fearful because of the spotlight now on them, dreading the hours that were about to be hoisted on their shoulders, and excited because this would be the largest case they'd ever been involved in.

So long as they kept focused, Tommy didn't care what they felt like.

"Do you need me anymore?" he said.

"No, I think we have everything you can give us. Thank you for your time, Special Agent Phillips."

"Sure," Tommy said, the calm taking back over. "I'm heading back to the condo, then to the office. We're going to stay in almost constant contact, okay? Anything you get, have a subordinate send it to all three of us immediately."

"Okay," Vadik said. "These agents that are coming, they have my number?"

"Yes," Luke said.

"All right, let's get to work," the other officer replied.

CHAPTER TWENTY

Luke walked through the condo with Tommy. Christian had left for the office to brief the other six agents on Ted Hinson and their job duties. Tommy was meticulously examining every inch of the condominium. Luke followed him from room to room, appearing to take in everything. His mind was passively categorizing what he saw, but that was only autopilot.

The brute force of Luke's brain concentrated on what was ahead.

Waverly's reaction hadn't been expected, and Luke felt annoyance at himself for not predicting it. He'd thought Waverly would act, but not *this* forcefully.

There was still much to be done, and now he had to deal with constant surveillance over a key piece. Tommy was silent as he walked through the condominium. Luke kept quiet, too. His mind was performing a blitzkrieg on the situation, following multiple lines of strategy at once to discern the best course of action.

Luke, for the first time in his life, wasn't sure he *had* a best course. He would make it out of this unscathed, and Mr. Hinson would end up dead, but the enterprise's overarching goal might be missed.

That couldn't happen.

Luke refused to allow it. He knew this was God's hand, moving against him as it always had. He didn't mind the hand. He enjoyed God's intervention most of the time.

However, this was a massive strike against Luke's purpose. God was trying to defeat everything he'd worked for, wiping the game board clean as if He was strong enough to do that. He wasn't.

Luke was stronger, and he would prove it by succeeding.

"What are you thinking?" Luke asked, the first words either of them had spoken since entering the condominium.

Tommy stood in the exact spot where Luke had put his arms around Alice's neck. "Everything is perfectly in place besides the fucking door. I can't even tell where she was grabbed, which makes no sense. There would have been a struggle. Something would have been disturbed."

He turned and looked at Luke. "You think it was Hinson? Do you really?"

"I think it's a strong probability."

"He didn't even *know* I was involved. He never met me. Never saw me. It would have made more sense for him to take Veronica, or Riley."

"Veronica hasn't been in Christian's life for quite some time. Riley and I haven't seen much of each other over the past few weeks, either, so it's possible he doesn't know about our relationships."

"But how would he know about mine?" Tommy asked.

"That's easier," Luke said. "If the man is vengeful, then all he had to do was follow us, or pay an investigator to do it so he wouldn't be seen. From there he sees you with us, and the investigator followed you and sees Alice."

"If it was a goddamn investigator, then he should come out now that her face is on every television station."

"I hope so," Luke said.

Tommy sighed. "Let's go back to the office. There's nothing we can do here."

The three took a break at Tommy's behest. They'd spent another six hours at the office, and he finally told them to go home, shower, and get some food.

"I'm fine," Christian said.

"You'll be here the rest of the night, and this is the only break you'll get."

Luke was grateful. He thought Tommy might want a few moments to himself, as he hadn't stopped since walking into his condominium the previous night.

Luke returned to his house, which was only fifteen minutes from the office. He didn't think this would take long. He didn't bother locking the door behind him. The shades were drawn across his living room windows, and he'd moved all his furniture back against the walls.

Last night, when Luke had left his house to meet Tommy, Alice had been sitting up straight in the chair.

Now, she and the chair were on the floor. Her head was resting on the floor, but she was still tied rigidly to the chair. She'd managed to scoot it maybe ten feet closer to the front door, but that was all.

She screamed through the cloth and tape over her mouth. No words, only rage, and her eyes showed the same. The veins and tendons in her neck stretched against her skin. She would kill Luke if let free, or give it her best shot.

Luke ripped the duct tape off in one quick movement.

"You motherfucker!" Alice screamed. *"Tommy's going to fucking kill you!"*

This was something else he hadn't expected. Two things in a single day. Luke hadn't thought Alice would contain such anger. Her personality over the years had given no indication of it. He had thought fear and pleading would be her natural response.

This unexpected emotion didn't matter, however. Luke was in control, and despite two unseen things in a day filled with millions of decisions, he would still succeed.

Alice panted to regain the oxygen lost from her muffled screams.

He grabbed another chair and placed it in front of Alice before sitting down. "You're very perceptive. You saw who I was at once last night. I'm impressed."

"Fuck you."

Luke nodded. "I understand why you feel that way."

"You're his goddamn partner! You've been with him for years!"

"I know. I know. This isn't personal, Alice. Not in the slightest. It's not even personal with Tommy. I'm telling you the truth when I say none of this has anything to do with you."

"Then why are you doing it? *Why the hell am I here, Luke?*"

"You're a piece in a much larger game. Larger than I have the time or desire to describe right now. Just know you're taking part in something much grander than your life could ever hope to be. Perhaps that can give you comfort with what comes next."

"What's going to happen?"

Luke stood and moved his chair back to its position against the wall. Alice's eyes followed him the whole time. He stepped back in front of her, twelve feet away. Her movement across the living room while he was gone gave him more space.

He took off his jacket and unholstered his weapon. "Do you believe in God, Alice?"

"Yes."

"Good. What happens next is you die, but since you believe in heaven, what happens after *that* should bring you comfort. Tommy dies. You can both be together again."

Alice opened her mouth to scream, but Luke moved too quickly. Her primal cry only lasted a split second before the bullet opened up the back of her skull.

She slumped and her bladder evacuated as her head lolled, her chin resting on the hardwood floor.

Luke carefully moved around the chair, keeping a wide berth, and looked at the blood spatter. None of it had touched his furniture or the walls. Only the hardwood floor, which was what he wanted. Easy cleanup. He glanced at the floorboard where the bullet had entered. Perhaps a subsonic hollow point would have been better, but he could fix the small hole.

Keeping his feet from touching any of the brain matter or blood splattered across the floor, he leaned forward and grabbed the back of the chair. Luke lifted it and carried it across the living room and into the foyer, then into his kitchen. He placed her out of the line of sight, so that if anyone came through the front door, they wouldn't see anything at first glance.

Luke walked back to the foyer and looked at the mess across his floor. He didn't have time to clean right now, and he didn't expect anyone to come to his house before he returned. Tonight he would move Alice's body to the needed location and throw a rug over his living room floor.

Now, though, he needed to return to the office. After all, the Bible said idle hands were the Devil's workshop.

"Fuck!" Tommy screamed. *"Fuck! Fuck! Fuck!"*

Christian looked out of the office window. People in their cubicles were standing up and looking into Tommy's office. They sat quickly once they saw him. It was no secret what was happening.

"What do you mean, you can't find him?" Luke asked, his voice a contrasting calm against Tommy's outburst.

"If he's in his house, his car isn't there. We've checked with the university, and he isn't at work today. We pressed them and they said he wasn't at work all week, and that he told them he needed another week off."

Tommy grunted. Christian thought another outburst

would follow, but he turned and slammed his hand against the wall.

"So what you're saying is, he's completely disappeared?" Tommy asked, his back to the speakerphone.

"So far. We contacted his cellphone provider, but they won't give us location information without a warrant. We've got it in front of a judge right now. Bridges and Prigam took it to him personally."

"Where are you right now?" Christian asked.

"We're on his street. Still watching the house."

Christian saw Tommy's eyes fall on him and he knew exactly what his partner was thinking. He shouldn't have stopped Christian last night.

Christian thought he saw something else in his face, too. He wondered if Luke saw it.

Tommy was going inside Hinson's house.

"Okay," Luke said. "Do you know when the judge will have a decision?"

"Should be within the hour."

"Call us back." Luke ended the call and looked at Tommy. His next words revealed that he saw the same as Christian. "If you go in there and she's not there, you're finished, Tommy. Just like you told Christian last night."

"And if she is there, I save her goddamn life." He turned to Christian. "You think it's him, too, don't you?"

Christian nodded, but something didn't feel exactly right about this. He hadn't been able to look at all the information his brain had processed over the past eighteen hours, and he hadn't entered his mansion. But the longer the day went on, the more *something* felt off.

Just like it had in John Presley's house.

"What are you thinking?" Tommy asked.

"It's got to be him," Christian answered. "There's no one else who would break into your home, take nothing, and kidnap her. It's got to be him giving us the middle finger."

"Then I'm going into *his* home. That's all there is to it."

"He's not there," Luke said.

"Did you check at the wife's house?" Tommy asked.

Luke nodded. "No one was home. I'm going back in a few hours."

Tommy was silent for a few seconds. "Alice might be at his place, even if he isn't."

"What if she's not? You're off the case. Most likely *she's* wherever *he* is. You don't want to hear this, but you need to. Hinson probably snapped, and this is bigger than a revenge kidnapping. He might not ever return to that house."

Tommy turned to the window again. "Then how do we find him?"

Christian agreed with Luke's logic, but Luke wasn't considering everything. "We can go in. If we find her, we save her. If we don't, no one has to know we went inside."

"What?" Tommy said.

"It's easy. You and I take over the surveillance tonight. We tell Waverly we want to see if we can catch something the other agents are missing. Then we pick the lock and go in. If he's in there, I'll kill him so you're clean. I was going to do it anyway. If he's not, we lock the door and get back in our car."

Tommy studied Christian's face carefully. "You think Waverly is going to let us get that close to him? He'll know I'm on edge."

Christian smiled. "Let me do the talking. I'm not on edge at all. I'm looking forward to killing the bastard."

Luke sat quietly while the other two spoke with Waverly. He'd lied about going over to Hinson's ex's house. He was going to, but he'd been able to buy himself some time when he told Waverly he'd check personally.

Ted Hinson and Christy Mackenrow had a child together. If Luke *hadn't* said he would be going over there, the FBI would have begun their surveillance of her, and rightfully so.

If Luke was a betting man, he would have put a lot of money on Dr. Hinson being at his ex-wife's house. He thought Dr. Hinson might have snapped, but he wasn't saying that to Tommy. A psychopath's mental state deteriorated over time. Their actions never fully satisfied their urges, and they continued wanting more.

Maybe Christian hadn't gone into his mansion to understand what was happening, but Luke had done his research.

The women had started going missing after Hinson's divorce. That's why they were still alive, or at least most of them were. Hinson was trying to replace his wife, and if one wife hadn't worked, then he would have multiple.

Yet, the blood stain Luke had seen in the basement showed Hinson's anger was getting the best of him. Perhaps, if Luke's luck held, he had finally snapped. Perhaps, Dr. Hinson had gone to Ms. Mackenrow's house in hopes of reclaiming his family.

Let his partners slip into Hinson's house alone, leaving him to find out where the man was.

If Tommy and Christian found the women locked in the basement? Well, they would manufacture a reason to have entered. Probably something along the lines of hearing someone scream. No one would say a word otherwise, not once Ted Hinson's true nature was discovered.

And then?

Well, they'd *all* be looking for Dr. Hinson and Alice.

Yes, Luke could set this up nicely. In the end, Christian would find that the spring weather trying to enter his life no longer existed. He'd find himself in a frozen prison forever.

CHAPTER TWENTY-ONE

Ted sat in his wife's living room. He no longer thought of Christy as his *ex-wife*. That was in the past, even if she didn't realize it yet.

Christy was being stubborn, just like she'd always been, but he could deal with that. Hell, he'd dealt with it for ten years before she'd finally left him. He would wait this stubbornness out.

It was Callie he worried about.

She sat next to him now, her red hair so pretty. Neither Ted nor Christy had red hair, and so when they'd first seen Callie's color, they both got a good laugh out of it. He had ribbed Christy, asking if Callie was really his child. Those had been good times.

Callie and Ted were sitting on the couch with the television on in front of them. He saw that she kept looking over at him, probably checking out the scratches on his face. At eleven years old, it was harder to lie to her, but he had told her a feral cat got into his house and scratched his face when he'd tried to capture it.

Ted wasn't completely sure she believed him, but she had no idea what had actually happened, which was all that mattered.

"Dad?" she asked.

"Yes, honey?" Ted didn't look away from the television. He loved this show, and while *Lockup* might not be suitable for someone Callie's age, he didn't mind letting her watch it.

"Is Mom coming home tonight?"

"No, not tonight, honey. I told you already. She's going to be home next Thursday."

"Why didn't we go to your house, then?"

"Well, first off, that cat really tore things up pretty bad, so the place isn't in the best condition. Second, she wanted me to watch over *this* house while she was gone."

Callie went quiet and turned back to the television.

The truth was a very different story. Ted had tied up Christy and put her in his trunk. They'd spent all day talking while Callie was at school, but she'd had to go back in the trunk once school was over.

Christy wasn't ready to see Callie yet. She was still ranting and raving, saying that Ted would be locked up in jail. Crazy talk. Everything was going to be just fine.

There was still the problem of the women in his basement, but now that he was with his wife and daughter it seemed like much less of a problem. He couldn't go home and clean everything up quite yet. He needed Christy to come around first. He thought by Thursday she'd see things his way.

"The people on this show are crazy," Ted said. "Always fighting over nothing."

Callie only nodded.

———

Luke chuckled as he pulled up a few houses down from Christy Mackenrow's house. So many people looking for Ted Hinson, and he was the only one here. His car was sitting in the driveway.

Unbelievable.

Luke had kept the rental car for a few more days. He couldn't drive his Tesla around right now, unfortunately. He stepped out of the rental and dropped the keys into his pocket. He had parked on the curb, not wanting to unnecessarily alert Hinson.

Luke stopped midway up the driveway.

He heard someone breathing. His eyes went to Dr. Hinson's car.

Oh, goodness, Luke thought. *You* have *snapped.*

He walked over to the trunk of the car, where the smallest sounds escaped. He tapped his knuckles twice on it.

Someone screamed and banged against the inside. The scream was heavily muffled. Luke imagined Dr. Hinson had used a gag very similar to the cloth and tape he had used on Alice. He tapped again and heard the same response.

Luke smiled and continued walking to the front door.

How far gone are you? he wondered as he reached the stoop. He would pick the lock if necessary, but he thought Mr. Hinson probably hadn't locked the door.

Why lock it when everything was going so well?

He turned the knob, and sure enough, it twisted easily in his hand.

Luke carefully opened the door. The house was silent, but he'd expected as much given that the lights were off. It was good to see Hinson and his daughter were keeping regular sleep hours.

No sense in letting a little murder get in the way of rest. That was how Luke saw it. He stepped inside without a sound and slowly shut the door. He *did* lock it.

Luke let his senses take over, processing everything that his eyes couldn't tell him. He smelled the little girl. The shampoo she used was different. Cheaper. He could smell the ex-wife, though she was fainter, meaning Ms. Mackenrow had been in that trunk for a little while.

He smelled Hinson, too. He was wearing the same cologne as the night in DC. Always wanting to look his best. Admirable.

Luke stepped into the living room, his eyes fully adjusted to the house's darkness. Hallways led from the left and right of the living room. Hinson's cologne took Luke left.

He walked in silence to the master bedroom. The door was open and he found Hinson lying on the bed with the covers pulled up to his neck.

Luke walked in and stood over the sleeping man, blocking out the moonlight and casting a shadow across Hinson's face.

"I told you I knew your name." His voice carried the perfect pitch to wake Hinson from his slumber.

Hinson's eyes snapped open and he blinked as he struggled to understand what was happening. He zeroed in on Luke.

"Whaaa…"

Luke smothered Hinson's face with a chloroform-drenched rag before he could say anything else and the house was silent once again.

Christian and Tommy stepped out of the vehicle, their hands already gloved. The night air was cool, but Christian left his jacket loose, wanting easy access to his weapon.

"You ready?" Tommy asked.

"I was ready last night."

"Shut up," Tommy said as he walked away.

Christian matched his pace and they went from the street to the driveway. Neither paused to look around and see if any nosey neighbors were watching.

It was midnight and the previous crew had left their post thirty minutes ago. Tommy and Christian had waited for half an hour, ensuring nothing else came up. The driveway had remained empty the entire time, and there had been no movement all day. Earlier, Tommy had instructed two other agents to wait outside the university in case Hinson went there.

No luck.

Christian wasn't concerned about luck now that he had Tommy on his side. This would end soon. If not tonight, then within the next twenty-four hours.

They headed around the back of the house after

deciding that was the safest entry point. Tommy tried the back door, but it was locked.

"Now we commit a crime," Tommy said. "Let's hope you're right about the alarm system."

"I am," Christian said from Tommy's right.

Ted Hinson didn't have an alarm system. Anyone who took women and held them in their house wouldn't want any chance that the police might arrive unannounced. An alarm system could accidentally call them, or if one of the women tried escaping, it wouldn't be hard for them to press the alert button.

Tommy moved to the window beside the door. Christian handed him the black towel he'd brought. Tommy wrapped it tightly around his hand, creating a barrier between him and the window. He positioned his fist about six inches from the glass pane and punched.

The glass shattered, briefly filling the night with noise as it fell to the floor inside.

Tommy used his wrapped hand to push out the remaining shards. Then he removed the towel and stuck his arm in and reached for the inside doorknob.

Christian heard the lock click as Tommy turned it.

They stepped into the house, not bothering to close the door. They stopped in the living room and listened. Neither spoke, nor heard anything from the house.

Tommy pulled out his flashlight with one hand and his weapon with the other. Christian unholstered his weapon as well, and they started their search.

They moved through the house, checking each room. Only one door wouldn't open.

"Who puts a padlock inside their house?" Christian asked, glaring at the locked door.

Tommy said nothing. He put the flashlight's end in his mouth and yanked on the padlock. It only jiggled against the clasp but didn't break.

"I'm going to call," he said, not looking at Christian.

"Go ahead."

"*Hello!*" he shouted.

Sarah heard the shout and cowered against the wall, shaking all over. She didn't make a sound. She couldn't tell if it was Ted shouting, or someone else.

She couldn't tell anything anymore. The four dead bodies in the basement with her were starting to smell. Her throat was like a desert, feeling like there was sand in her esophagus instead of saliva. She had urinated in her pants, although the lack of food kept her from soiling herself.

Sarah kept her eyes shut, squeezing them tightly so that nothing could get in.

"*This is the FBI! Is anyone down there?*"

Sarah shook her head. It wasn't the FBI. It was Ted, testing her. Trying to see if she meant what she'd told him. If she shouted back, begging for help, he would come down and do the same to her as he had the other women.

She kept shaking her head, refusing to make a sound. Ted hadn't been here in a long time and now he was trying to trick her. He wanted her to make a mistake and then it would all be over.

"*If anyone's down there, this is the FBI!*"

Sarah put her hands to her ears, trying to block out the lying voice from above.

"We can break in," Christian said.

Tommy looked at the padlock, his flashlight shining on it. "We don't have the tools."

"Think you can kick it in?"

Tommy had already considered it. The padlock was placed six inches from the top of the door, meaning that he couldn't break the frame where the lock was fixed. Kicking the door would dent it. Perhaps he'd even kick through it, but that would only leave a hole with one of his legs stuck inside it.

"I don't think so."

"Then we go get tools."

"Okay, slow down. I need to think for a second."

He walked away from the door, not waiting to see if Christian followed. He sat on the living room couch. Christian came and stood in front of him.

"If she's down there, we would have heard her even if her mouth is taped shut. So, she's either down there and knocked out or..." Tommy looked at Christian, darkness shrouding his features. He couldn't finish the sentence. "If we break into that room and find nothing, when Hinson returns, it's over. He'll see we were here and kill her immediately."

"We could wait for him to show up." Christian paused for a second. "I need some time to think if you want any better ideas."

"Let me call Luke," Tommy said.

***

Luke looked at Tommy's name on his phone. He hit answer and put it to his ear.

"Any progress?" he asked as he looked down at the frightened Dr. Hinson.

The man was unbound on the couch, completely docile. Instead of using duct tape and a sock, Luke had stuck the barrel of his pistol in Hinson's mouth. It was keeping him very quiet.

"No," Tommy said. "He's not here. There's a door with a padlock on it. No sounds from below and I can't kick it in."

"Bolt cutters?" Luke suggested.

"We've thought about it, but if there's no one there, when Hinson returns, he'll kill Alice once he sees we've been there."

"He's not going to see that already? With the glass broken?"

"That'll be less obvious. We'll clean up the glass and lock the door. He won't notice it immediately."

Luke watched Hinson try to adjust his mouth around the barrel, his teeth grinding against the metal. "Your shift is over at four?"

"Yeah."

"Let's meet at the office and figure out what options we have."

"Luke..." Tommy's voice broke with raw emotion. A second passed before he continued. "Do you have any ideas? Anything you can think of that might help?"

"I may," Luke said. "Stay at the house and we'll meet back at the office shortly, okay?"

"Okay," Tommy said, clearly still struggling to keep his emotions in check.

"Tommy?" Luke said.

"Yeah?"

"It's going to be okay. We'll find her. I promise."

"Okay, Luke. Okay. Thanks."

Luke hung up and placed his phone back in his pocket. He removed the gun from Hinson's mouth slowly, not wanting to chip any of his teeth.

"Okay, that should give us a few hours." Luke sat in the chair opposite Hinson. "How are you feeling?"

Hinson said nothing. His lower lip quivered.

Luke ignored his fear. "I have a few things I need to clean up before I head back to the office, so I don't have a lot of time right now, Dr. Hinson. It's important that you listen to me, so that we are both on the same page."

Sweat dripped from Hinson's brow into his eyes. He wiped the salty water away, remaining silent.

"Your daughter is still asleep, which is good. Whatever we do, we don't want to wake her yet, okay? What time does she normally get up?"

"I-I-I don't know," the man stammered.

"Not the best father, I see. Okay, we're going to play it safe and say six. That means everything we have to do needs to be finished by then. I promise you, Dr. Hinson. If she interrupts our endeavors, I will kill her immediately. She is less than inconsequential to me. Do you understand?"

Hinson nodded.

"You love her, don't you?"

Another nod.

"And your ex-wife?"

Another nod.

"I believe you," Luke said. "Your love is the desperate kind, and sometimes that causes pain for others. That's okay. We'll fix it all by tomorrow. Sound good?"

Hinson nodded once again, being led along like a small puppy following someone holding a treat.

"If you want to live, Dr. Hinson, you'll need to do everything I say, and exactly as I say it. I'm going outside to get your wife. Where are your keys?"

He lifted a shaking hand and pointed toward the kitchen counter.

Luke didn't look away from Hinson's eyes. "I'm going outside to get your wife out of the trunk. I know you're scared right now. However, when I walk out, that fear may dissipate and you might forget how dangerous I am. You need to know in your soul that I'm more lethal than you can imagine, and if you move so much as an inch from this spot in the two minutes I'm gone, I will take your face off and feed it to you."

Hinson swallowed. "Okay. I won't."

"Won't what?"

"W-w-won't move."

"Good," Luke said. "You're stuttering like someone else I used to know. Let's hope your end is better than hers. I'll be back."

Luke went to the counter and took the keys lying where Hinson had pointed. He walked outside and opened the trunk of Hinson's car.

The trunk's light temporarily blinded the woman inside. She fought through the pain quickly and squinted Luke. She screamed through the tape around her mouth.

"Hi, Ms. Mackenrow. We're going to go inside now."

The woman screamed again and Luke nodded.

"I know you'll want to make some noise, so forgive me for this." Luke slammed his palm directly into her forehead. She slumped back down to the trunk's bottom.

Luke looked at the red mark and decided it wouldn't leave a bruise. He picked the woman up like a bride, then closed the trunk with his elbow and carried the unconscious woman back into the house.

Hinson had kept his word. Sweat was falling from his forehead, but he was in the same spot. Luke didn't think he'd moved *at all*, not even a finger. He laid the woman down on the floor at the living room's entry. "Okay, Dr. Hinson, your whole family is here now. How many people have you killed?"

"Wha-What?"

"People. How many have you killed since you started this?" Luke saw the man trying to decide if his fear of admitting how many he'd killed was greater than his fear of Luke.

He realized Luke was much more dangerous than sharing information. "Fuh-Five."

Luke smiled. "Let's see if we can add to that body count."

CHAPTER TWENTY-TWO

Christian and Tommy exited the elevator on their floor of the FBI building. They turned the lights on since no one else was there. Christian was exhausted, and he knew Tommy felt the same, but they wouldn't be done until they had Alice back.

"I'm going to start making calls," Tommy said. "See what everyone else found. Let me know when Luke gets here, okay?"

"Yeah, sure," Christian said.

Tommy went to his office, leaving Christian alone.

Christian walked to his office and collapsed in his chair. He leaned his head back. He needed a nap. A short one. Ten minutes. His mind was struggling to keep up with the demands he was forcing on it, and if it didn't get some rest, even just a few minutes, he would be useless to Tommy.

Christian set an alarm on his phone and closed his eyes.

Christian knew almost immediately that he was dreaming he was in his mansion. It wasn't the mansion that gave it away. He knew it was a dream because Luke was in front of him.

Excluding the Other's presence in this place, there had never been anyone else. Luke couldn't gain entry unless this was a dream.

"It is a dream," Luke said.

Christian nodded, not knowing what else to do. A sharp sense of unease ran through him. It permeated the air, and when he breathed, it filled him as well.

"Why am I dreaming we're here?" Christian heard himself ask, though he wasn't in control.

Aren't I supposed to be in charge when lucid dreaming? he wondered.

"Not this one," Luke said. "Your mind didn't have any other way to reach out, I suppose. It hasn't been able to slow you down. You've been neglecting for so long what it's been building, that it finally reached out and grabbed you. Consider this another one of your movies, Christian."

Luke turned and walked across the foyer, heading for the double staircase that split and wrapped around the opposite sides of the circular walls.

Christian followed, his legs controlled by something other than him. His mind, perhaps, but not the conscious part.

Neither spoke as they climbed the stairs, and Christian saw that the staircase went higher than he remembered.

Not remembered, he thought. *It's higher than you built it.*

"It is," Luke said. "There's a new floor at the top."

The two kept climbing. Time was different, as it always

was in dreams. Christian couldn't tell how long they'd been going up. He could see the distance. The last floor Christian remembered building had cut off two stories ago, but still the staircases wrapped upward. They were now following a vertical tunnel with huge, life-size paintings on the walls.

All of them were of Christian and his partners. The farther up they went, the more the paintings focused on Luke, showing him as Christian had seen him at different times. Sitting in his living room. In Christian's own office. Hanging upside down on a makeshift cross, convincing Christian to force Lucy Speckle to suicide.

Finally, the stairs ended, and they took the last step onto a vast floor.

Does it even end? Christian thought.

"There," Luke said, and pointed to the ceiling.

Christian followed his gesture and saw a final painting. It stretched across the entire ceiling; Luke Titan reigned over this floor. Christian had to move his head to see the entire thing, and even then, Luke's feet were too far away to see well. The painting showed Luke in one of his three-piece suits. His hands were at his sides, and his eyes stared *directly* at Christian.

Christian walked across the floor without looking away from the painting, and Luke's eyes moved to follow him. His brown irises stared out as if they were alive, each eye large enough for Christian to lie across and not cover them.

"You need to come to this place," Luke said.

Christian looked back down and saw his partner had turned and was staring at him.

"It's important that you do."

"This…is real?" Christian spoke, and it was him this time, not something else controlling his words.

Luke nodded. "Yes. This is inside your mansion, and it's important you see it."

"Why?"

"Everything you care about depends upon it, Christian. Perhaps it always has."

The alarm on Christian's clock sounded with a ferocity that broke the dream into pieces. It fell away, leaving reality to stare back at him.

Christian sat up in his office chair, trying to remember what he'd seen.

Luke. The staircase stretching upward.

You need to come to this place.

Luke rapped his knuckles on Christian's door. Christian blinked rapidly, returning to the world around him. Luke opened the door and Christian knew he didn't want this man in his office. He didn't want to be anywhere near Luke.

He didn't know why, only that it was so, and no amount of thought or logic would make it otherwise.

"I wanted to ask you how Tommy's doing before we go down there," Luke said as he approached Christian's desk. He glanced at the still buzzing phone. "Taking a nap?"

Christian grabbed his phone and hit the stop button, feeling a need to hide the alarm. He didn't want Luke to know what he'd seen in the dream, but feared that Luke might somehow know.

"Are you okay?" Luke asked.

"Yes. I just woke up. Sorry. We're all run ragged, worrying about Tommy, and Alice."

"No need to apologize," Luke said. "How is Tommy?"

Christian wanted to run from the room, to jump out of the window behind him if necessary. Anything to get away from the man standing there. He'd never felt fear like this. His heartbeat thumped in his ears, his pulse thundering rapidly.

Don't let him know you're afraid, Christian thought.

But that was impossible. Luke was too perceptive.

"Are you sure you're all right?" Luke asked.

Christian nodded. "Yes, you just startled me. Tommy… Tommy's trying to hold it together. Let's go to his office. He told me to let him know when you got here."

Luke stared at him, waiting on him to stand.

"You mind giving me a minute?" Christian asked. "I need to clear my head."

"Sure," Luke said, but he paused a moment longer and stared at Christian.

Christian held his gaze, but it took a will matching that of the Pharaohs building the Egyptian pyramids. He wanted to look away, even to beg Luke to leave. Anything that would get him out of this office, *away* from him.

Finally, Luke turned and exited without saying anything.

Christian sighed.

"What the hell was that?" he asked himself.

You need to come to this place.

Christian didn't have time, not at the moment. He knew Tommy was expecting him shortly, and he also needed to hear what Luke had to say. If there was a plan to save Alice, Luke would have it.

His heart still was beating far too rapidly, but he stood from his desk and did his best to push away the crippling fear.

"How are you holding up?" Luke said.

He didn't care about Tommy's answer. His mind was on the interaction with Christian moments ago. Luke didn't like what he'd seen. The boy had been positively frightened —terrified, even.

"I'm okay. Where's Christian?" Tommy asked.

"He's on his way. I think he took a nap. He was just waking up when I went to his office."

Tommy nodded. "I spoke to the police. They've been questioning Alice's friends and family. They've got nothing so far, and no other leads. The FBI agents the director assigned to the case are going back to my condo to rein-spect the crime scene. They want to see if the police missed anything."

"You think that's a waste of time?" Luke asked.

What was Christian frightened of? The entire endeavor going on around him? Alice was in danger, but that didn't make much sense as an explanation, especially given what the boy had experienced the past few years.

"Probably. I don't know where else to send them."

Tommy looked up from his desk and Luke turned to

see Christian arriving. His skin was pale and Luke noted the slight tremor in his right hand.

"You don't look good," Tommy said.

"I took a nap and had a nightmare. It's taking me a minute to shake it."

Tommy nodded but said nothing else about it, turning to Luke. "Tell me you have something."

"We need to go back to Hinson's ex-wife's," Luke said as Christian took his seat. "I checked again, but it might be time to sit on the house."

Tommy sighed. "We need to tell Waverly, then we'll go over there."

Luke watched him regain his focus, pure force of will shrugging off the exhaustion and self-hate. His will to slug forward like a knight facing insurmountable enemies was admirable, but it wouldn't save him in the end. Going forward only because duty and love demanded it.

Could he still go forward knowing that he and everything he cared for was already lost?

Not yet, old friend, but soon, Luke thought. He wanted to scrutinize Christian, but he didn't. Staring too hard at the boy wasn't good, but Luke wasn't exactly sure why. *That* annoyed him, not knowing why, while knowing it to be true. It was as if...

Christian had been *scared of him.*

Tommy hit the button on his speakerphone and dialed Waverly's cell.

"Hold on," the director answered. He clicked the mute button and thirty seconds passed before he came back on the line. "Sorry, I'm in a meeting. What do you have?"

"I'm here with Luke and Christian. Sir, we haven't been

able to find his ex-wife, so a tail on her house may be in order."

"Okay. Twenty-four hour surveillance on her, too. I'll reassign six more agents. When was the last time any of you went over?"

"Yesterday evening," Luke said. "Still no answer, sir."

"It's 5AM now," Waverly said. "Get over there by 6:30. If she's there, tell her whatever you need to ensure that she cooperates with the surveillance. Tell her what we suspect and that she might be in danger. Figure out if she knows where Hinson might be. Any news from the police?"

"Nothing useful, sir," Tommy said.

"If you have the capacity, direct some of the agents following Hinson to start looking into all his friends and family. It's time to widen the investigation. If you need more people, let me know, okay?"

"We will," Tommy said.

"Okay. I have to go," the director said. "Call me once you've made contact with the ex-wife."

"Yes, sir," Tommy said.

The line went dead, leaving the three partners sitting in silence.

"We've got an hour and a half," Tommy said. He stood from his chair and stretched his hands high above his head, ligaments popping in his shoulders. "I'm going to finish reading these reports. We'll go meet the ex-wife in an hour, okay?"

"I think one of us should stay on Hinson," Christian said. "Someone should be with the agents watching his house. If he goes there, they might not move like we'd want them to. If we're there, we'll be able to command the situation better."

Tommy said nothing, and Luke let himself turn toward Christian. The boy was still pale, although the tremor had stopped. "Are you sure that's a good idea? Having one of us watch the house seems like a waste of time, especially with what we need to be doing."

"Think about it," Christian said. "If he shows up, the agents will call it in, but they're not going to move on him. If one of us is there, we can convince them to move in, even if we have to take the blame later."

Tommy nodded reluctantly. Luke thought Tommy didn't like the idea, and neither did he, but for very different reasons. Christian's suggestion held *some* logic, but it wasn't very strong. Luke didn't understand why he would say it, especially with such force.

"You want to do it?"

"No," Christian said. "I want to meet his ex-wife. It might help with the mansion."

Tommy shrugged. "Luke? It's not a bad idea to take a few hours with them in case he shows up."

Luke stared at Christian, not caring if it set the boy off again. He wanted Christian to feel pressure, perhaps even to *cause* a panic attack. Something was happening here, and he didn't like it. Christian didn't return his gaze, keeping his eyes on Tommy.

"Luke? You still here?"

"Sure," he said to Tommy. "I'll go with them."

CHAPTER TWENTY-THREE

Christian knew the plan of action wasn't smart given Luke's brainpower. It was a waste putting him in a car to watch an empty house. If anyone should go, it was Tommy, but Christian didn't want that.

He'd made the suggestion because he needed distance from Luke, desperately so...*and* he needed time to think. He needed time to go to his mansion, but what waited for him on that upper floor would take *a lot* of time to process.

Christian was scared to go into the mansion. He was afraid, as he had been before, of what he might find.

No...that wasn't accurate. He was scared of what he *would* find.

He *did* want to see Hinson's ex-wife. It would add something to the mansion and when he went to it, he wanted all possible information to be waiting. However, he wanted to see everything in one inspection. He was too frightened of the place to make more than one trip.

How did it come this far? That you're afraid of what used to be your sanctuary?

Christian went to his office and set another alarm. He didn't know if he would dream what he needed, but he thought it was better than going inside. At least right now.

He leaned back in his chair and sleep came quickly. He found himself in his mansion again, but inside the room marked *The Priest*.

The statues were still there, the women in different states of prostration before himself… Wait, no. The statue of Christian had been replaced by the Other.

The wild grin was still on his face and blood leaked from the corners of his eyes, falling down his cheeks and to his neck in awful, endless streams.

"You dreamed of Luke," the Other said. "Now you're dreaming of me. What do you think that means?"

Christian found himself in control again. The Other looked around at the statues. He shook his head violently and the bloody tears sprinkled on the stone sculptures.

"You're going insane," Christian said.

The Other laughed, a manic cackle that filled the room. "And you aren't? I am you, Christian. You are me. You keep this mental barrier as if it matters, but we both know it doesn't. Not in the end. Our destiny is to grow into one."

Christian didn't try denying what the Other said. From his replica's first appearance, Christian knew it to be true. He had momentarily thought he could break free when he went to Hinson's house the previous night, intent on killing the man. That chance was gone, though.

"It's not gone, my man. You can still kill him. You might even be able to kill him at his ex-wife's house. But when you kill him now, it'll be our marriage. Things have changed in the past few days, and your separation from me is over. It's you and I to the end." The Other smeared his fingers through the blood running down his face, then leaned forward and traced twin red tracks down Christian's face. "That's better. The outside matches the inside."

He looked into Christian's eyes. "Do you think that once you kill Hinson, you'll ever be able to sleep next to Veronica again? In the end, Hinson is finished, and you know it. Waverly is onboard with Hinson as a killer. If you murder him now, you're doing it for yourself. You're not doing it for Waverly. The thing that makes me chuckle… But you know what that is, don't you?"

Christian nodded. "I won't be able to stop myself."

"Exactly. You'll murder him because you want him dead, and it's not necessary any longer. He'll spend his life in jail or take a ride on old sparky, if you let him live. But you won't. He's going to die and you're going to enjoy it. Then, Christian, as your friend Luke analogized, the winter will be here forever."

Christian wanted to say he was wrong, but that would be futile. While everything in Christian's life besides Veronica was wrong, what the Other said was right.

"*Nail on the head!*" the Other screeched with a horrible gale of laughter.

"Why did you come here?" Christian said.

"*That* is the question. The one you never really tried to answer. Now it's too late, isn't it? You don't have the time to chase down the answer. You barely have time to sleep. I wonder how rested you'll feel when you leave here?"

The Other's smile died, and Christian was staring at a reflection of himself.

It was shocking, seeing the Other without the maniacal

aura he always radiated. Christian had to accept that he *was* looking at himself. Communicating with himself.

Fine snowflakes began to fall around them, then the Other's eyes went fully black. His pupils swam out across his irises and covered the surrounding white.

Christian stared wordlessly into the dark orbs reflecting *him*. A different man than the one who had first joined the FBI.

"Before we're married, Christian, I'd answer that question. I'd do it before you kill someone. When that happens… Well, it *will* be too late, then."

―――――

The sun was ascending above the neighborhood's houses. Luke sat in the backseat of the car, while the other two agents were in the front of the vehicle.

Luke didn't need to be at Ms. Mackenrow's house, and thought showing his face there wasn't a great idea. Seeing Hinson again might create a bit too much stress on the actor and actresses in this play.

Yet, it hadn't been *his* idea to end up in the back of this car, watching a house that held nothing of interest—at least not for Luke. The FBI agents might find the house's basement interesting, but in reality, those women were merely bit players.

Luke knew he needed time alone with Christian, but he also knew he wouldn't get it. All his brainpower, and he couldn't figure out where Christian's strange fear had originated from. Every path his mind followed led to only one answer, although it was impossible.

Christian Windsor knew Luke was behind all this. He knew Luke had been behind *everything*.

That couldn't be. Nothing had changed. Perhaps the boy did have a nightmare, and that's all this was.

But you're the one sitting in a car doing grunt work, Luke thought. *That's not part of your plan.* This *is Christian's plan.*

Or was it God's? Was this another movement of His hand, an effort to rearrange the game's pieces and giving Him yet another unfair advantage?

Luke was powerful enough to withstand it. His plan would win out, and then, he would be one step closer to achieving his purpose.

He pulled out a small notepad from his pocket and began writing another letter.

FOR CHRISTIAN WINDSOR

Dear Christian,

When you break evolution down, adaptation is its primary essence. At the beginning of these letters, I said that you would die soon after reading them. A trait that has allowed me to move around this world with such ease, is that I readily adapt to changing circumstances. That is what separates the species that die off from those that thrive, the ability to adapt.

I no longer want you to die. Your remaining life will be a testament to God's failure. As he looks down from his throne, he'll see you and know he lost another round between the two of us.

You're going to survive this, and so that means I must find a different way to give you these letters. It certainly wouldn't behoove me to give you them in their current form. That would ruin all of my detailed planning.

Do not fret, though. I will figure it out.

I told you that my next letter would describe my hate for God, but I've also changed my mind on that point. You're going to live, and I think it appropriate to give you goals while you sit knowing I did what is coming.

I won't hide my purpose from you. That will come before this chapter in your life closes. However, the goal I set out for you is to understand why I have this purpose.

Find out why I hate God, Christian.

The search may not fill a life, but it'll help pass the time, I'm sure.

Yours,

Luke Titan, MD, PhD, Special Agent for the Federal Bureau of Investigations

CHAPTER TWENTY-FOUR

Tommy knocked hard on the door.

"Why don't we ever ring the doorbell?" Christian said.

Tommy looked at his partner. He shook his head and turned back to the door. "I'll never understand you."

Christian said nothing else while the two waited.

A minute passed with no answer. Tommy knocked again, longer and harder.

Finally, they heard a lock turn and the door opened. A woman stood before them in a long robe, looking as though she had been up long enough to run a brush through her hair. Her skin was pale, though, and large, dark bags sat beneath her eyes.

"Can I help you?"

"Good morning, ma'am. We're with the Federal Bureau of Investigation. I'm Special Agent Thomas Phillips, and this is my partner, Special Agent Christian Windsor. We'd like to speak to you about your ex-husband."

"I have to get ready for work right now. I don't have time."

Tommy had opened his mouth ready to say "thank you," fully expecting to be let inside. Her refusal had him staring, unable to find any words.

"Ms. Mackenrow," Christian said, taking up the slack. "This is extremely important. Your boss will understand your tardiness once you explain why you're late. We believe you and your daughter are in danger from your ex-husband."

The woman's lower lip trembled. She broke eye contact and looked down at her feet. Tommy saw her swallow, but when she looked back up the tremble was gone.

"Ted isn't a danger to me or my daughter. He loves us both. Now, I really don't have time to talk. I'm already running late. If there's something you need from me, you can contact my lawyer."

Tommy didn't need a bright neon sign hanging from the house, flashing *TROUBLE* to know things were very, very wrong here.

"Ms. Mackenrow, you're acting peculiarly," Tommy said, determined to use as much force as needed to have a conversation with this woman. "We just told you that you and your daughter are in danger, and you're telling me you're late for work." He paused and his next words came out in a low whisper. "Nod if something is wrong here."

A blankness spread across the woman's face, as if someone had wiped the hard drive of her mind. She didn't nod, and didn't glance away, either. "I don't know what you're talking about, but I'd like you to leave. You can contact my lawyer if you have a problem. His name is Pete Tranch."

"Ma'am—" Tommy was cut off when she closed the door in his face.

He looked at Christian. Neither moved from the stoop.

"What the fuck?" Tommy whispered.

"Let's go," Christian said. "Now."

Christy Mackenrow stood staring at the door she had just closed. The blank stare that had taken over her face disappeared the same moment as the FBI agents. Tears streamed from her eyes, but she didn't dare make a sound. She didn't move for a few seconds, only stood there crying.

She knew she had to go back to the bedroom. Ted was waiting, and so was Callie. She trudged across the house, her feet barely lifting an inch off the floor. She had no idea what was going on, only that she and her daughter were more than "in danger" as the FBI agent had put it. They were one mistake away from death, and all that mattered was ensuring her daughter remained alive.

Christy reached the bedroom door. Ted was on the bed. He held a gun to their daughter's head. She could barely look at Callie, knowing that if she stared too long she'd lose control.

Callie's mouth was taped shut. Ted hadn't done *that*. The other man had. The one from last night who had knocked her out before bringing her inside.

Christy hadn't heard what the man and Ted had spoken about, but when she woke, life was even more precarious than when Ted had arrived.

Ted had originally told her they were getting back

together and shoved her in that fucking trunk. He'd spent the night with Callie, treating her well.

Now, he held a gun to Callie's head.

"Are they gone?" he asked.

"Yes."

"Good. Go sit in the living room."

Christy stared for another second at her daughter. "It's going to be okay, honey."

Callie broke out in fresh tears and Christy hated herself for causing them. She left the room, knowing that if she stayed, Ted would kill his daughter.

Ted put the gun down on the bed. He stared at it as if it were a malformed animal with two heads dying in front of him, unable to support the monstrosity of its life.

It wasn't his gun.

It's not mine, he thought. *None of this. This isn't my fault. It's not. It's not. It's not.*

Callie tried to run, but Ted grabbed her shoulder and pulled her back to the bed.

"No, honey," he said, though he didn't look at her. He *couldn't* look at her. He couldn't look at any of this. It shouldn't be happening.

He wasn't supposed to be sitting on a bed holding a pistol to his daughter's head. To *Callie's* head.

Ted knew he could stop it. He could call the police and put an end to everything, but Luke Titan had made it very clear what would happen if he did.

"I've been to your house, Dr. Hinson. I've seen what's in

your basement. I imagine things might have changed since then, given that you're here now. The moment you start thinking I'm not dangerous, and you try to start cleaning up your mess, you'll be caught. Right now FBI agents are watching your house, and they'll come to this one tomorrow."

Ted had stared at him, his lower lip quivering as the reality of the situation spilled from the man's mouth.

"You had some fun with those women, didn't you? *Sexual* fun. Do you know what they do to rapists in jail? I'm sure you do, so I won't delve into the dirty details. If you try cleaning this up, you will spend the rest of your days in prison with men twice your size who *hate* rapists. But if you listen to me, you'll make it out of this without any problems. Your ex-wife, or should I say wife? Either way, she'll need to die. Your daughter may live if you can make sure she stays quiet. If not, she'll have to go as well. However, the bright spot in all this is you will make it out alive, and as a free man."

Ted focused on that last sentence as he stared at the gun.

You will make it out alive, and as a free man.

He hated himself for it, but that was all he cared about. He couldn't go to jail, and he knew Titan was telling the truth. Titan *was* the FBI.

"It'll be okay, honey," Ted said absently. "It'll all be okay."

Make it out alive, and as a free man.

He just had to follow Titan's instructions for a few more hours.

CHAPTER TWENTY-FIVE

"He's gotten to her, too," Tommy said.

Christian sat in the passenger seat, hearing his partner but not paying attention.

"We need to get inside."

Christian said nothing.

"Are you listening to me, man? He's in there with Alice, and that woman and her daughter are being held hostage. There's no doubt about it."

"Tommy…" Christian paused. He knew his next few words would be hard for Tommy, and for once in his life, he was measuring his communication before speaking. "I need you to trust me, okay?"

"Whatever you want to say, get it out now. We don't have time for pussy-footing around."

"I need you to take me home. I need about three hours to myself."

"What are you talking about?" Tommy asked. "There's no time for you to go off and start searching your mansion.

That man is in there with my fiancée. We're going in now, and we're going to put a fucking bullet in his head. We'll figure out our story afterwards, but we're not waiting around for anything else. Do you understand?"

Christian looked at his partner. "In three hours, if I don't have what I'm looking for, we'll go in. I promise. You know I don't care about that. I'm done with the FBI after this. I need three hours, though."

"Don't do this, Christian." Tommy's eyes filled with tears. "Not right now. I can't fucking handle it and we don't have *time*."

"I'm sorry, but I have to. Do you think I'd ask you this otherwise? If you want Alice back, I need this time. He won't kill her in three hours. Just pull away from the house and take me home."

"You don't know he won't! He knows we're after him!"

Christian didn't look away. "Nothing that is happening makes sense, Tommy. I've been so focused on finding Alice that I didn't think about it before. Hinson took your fiancée? Why? If anything, he would have gone after Luke or me. Not you. It was a stupid theory from the beginning. Something is happening here, but it's not what we think, and I need time to figure it out."

Tommy looked back to the house. He reached up and wiped the tears from his eyes. "If she dies in the next three hours, Christian…"

"I know. Trust me, please."

Tommy swallowed. "You better be right. You better be goddamn right."

"I think I am. One other thing, Tommy?"

"What?" His partner didn't look over to him.

"Don't answer Luke's calls, and don't go near him."

Christian waited until Tommy pulled away. He watched the car roll down the road and exit his neighborhood. He didn't have five minutes to spare waiting on an Uber, and he still hadn't turned in the FBI cruiser he checked out two days ago. He had only asked Tommy to drop him off here so that he could drive alone. He pulled the keys from his pocket and got into the car.

It didn't take long to reach Luke's house. Christian punched in the gate code and drove the car onto the massive driveway. Luke's car wasn't there, so he parked where the Tesla usually resided.

He stepped from the vehicle and looked at the house. The shades were drawn across the living room. Christian had never seen that before. Luke always kept them open.

"Why, Luke? Why close them today?" Christian asked the still air. No answer came, just as none had for quite some time.

How long? he wondered. *How long has it been since a real answer came to you?*

But he didn't need to search for *that* answer. Since Lucy Speckle. That was the last time he'd been free in his mind.

Christian walked to the front door, keys in hand. Luke had trusted him with a key, just as Christian had trusted Luke, and now...what? What was he doing here?

He didn't know precisely, but his actions didn't spring from trust. Christian was certain of that.

He put the key in the lock and turned. The door opened. Luke had no alarm system. Nothing could ever touch him. That was how he looked at life, so why waste money frivolously?

Christian stepped into the foyer. He looked into the kitchen, but saw nothing out of the ordinary. He turned into the living room as he had so many times before, although this was the first time he'd been here without Luke.

He stopped in the doorway, looking at the new addition.

Christian stared at the large rug that covered nearly the entire floor. Luke would never sully his space with something like this. He prided himself on his design capabilities, even if he didn't speak of them. Each piece of this house had been carefully selected, especially the hardwood floors.

Christian walked to the rug's edge and squatted. He touched the fabric, immediately knowing that while it had no place here, Luke hadn't scrimped on cost. It was thick, and soft to the touch, something he'd like to walk across barefoot.

"Why is this here?" he wondered.

"Why are you here?" his mother asked. She stood on the rug, a few feet in front of him.

Christian looked up at her, but she said nothing else. That was the question. Why *had* he come here?

Because of his dream. The top floor that his mind would no longer hold back, forcing it on him through his dreams. He still hadn't gone to it, though he'd have to very soon. He had asked for three hours, and that's all Tommy would give him.

Who was behind Alice's investigation? From the beginning, it had been Luke. He had taken control because Tommy was too emotional, even if he didn't show it.

What had Luke told him about Ted Hinson? He'd given Christian permission to kill the man, to do whatever his heart desired. He'd cloaked it in faith, but the reality was that Luke had encouraged Christian to kill. And he nearly had.

What about Hinson's ex-wife? Who had said they would handle her? Luke, who had said no one had been home. Except what had happened when they arrived at the house?

Mackenrow had answered the door. She'd oscillated between being a nervous wreck and a zombie freshly risen from death. They'd gone to her house *after* Luke suggested it. What if Christian had thought about her first? Would the same thing have played out?

Where was Luke when Alice went missing?

Where was Tommy? Chasing Christian down in front of Ted Hinson's lawn.

He pulled his cellphone out and called Tommy.

"Are you ready?" his partner answered.

"Not yet. Soon. I need you to tell me the truth now, Tommy. Alice's life may depend on it. Did Luke tell you I was going to Hinson's house the other night? Or did you figure it out on your own?"

"What the hell does that have to do with anything?"

"Just answer me," Christian said. His voice was calm, his free hand still rubbing the soft rug.

"He told me. We'd been watching you for a few days. He

said you would do it soon. What does that matter? What's it have to do with Alice?"

"Two more hours, Tommy. Just two."

Christian hung the phone up and turned it off. He didn't want any interruptions.

Luke had lied to him.

Not quite, he thought, his mind replaying what Luke had said. He wouldn't tell anyone, not until the time is right.

Always so careful with your words. Whose time, is the question. Yours or mine?

Christian stood and walked across the rug to the couch. He sat, finally ready to see what resided at the top of his mansion.

Christian first headed to Luke's room. His mind had built it near the first two psychopaths' when he'd first met Luke.

A sign hung from the doorknob, a metal string hooking through two holes on either side. It read, "Relocated to top floor. Sorry for any inconvenience." Christian would have laughed if he wasn't so frightened.

He made his way to the staircase and started climbing. The stairs went much higher than the last time he was *actually* here.

But you've been up them before, even if not consciously, he thought.

Finally he reached the top. There were no more steps to take and he could ascend no higher. Christian's dream had been accurate. The painting of Luke covered the ceiling above, stretching over the entire floor. Christian focused on the eyes, and sure enough, they looked back at him.

The floor was open and vast. Christian stared at it for a second, honestly impressed at what his mind had accomplished. The rest of his mansion held rooms, each one dedicated to specific people or events. Inside each room was everything his mind knew about the person or event, with his mother's being the largest. He'd spent almost three decades knowing his mother, and even her room was smaller than this.

Her area was still a room. Luke Titan had a whole floor dedicated to him.

"How did I not see this?" he asked.

"I think you'll understand the answer once you explore a bit," the Other said.

He was farther down the steps, but Christian heard his footfalls climbing from behind. Christian didn't turn around, but the Other's voice sounded different, somehow. Perhaps even sad.

Christian walked forward, ignoring the eyes above him that were following his every movement. He didn't know where to begin. The place was just too *large*.

"I'd go right," the Other said. "Though, if you want to jump to the end, head left. It moves chronologically." The Other was now on the floor but not coming any closer.

Christian went right, wanting to understand the full scope of what lay before him. The floor's walls were all digital, but something new had been added. They also projected holograms.

The first section of wall showed a video of Christian

meeting Luke. Tommy was there, too. The video didn't show the interaction from Christian's point of view, however.

He saw it from Luke's.

"This is how Luke sees the world?" he asked the Other.

"Yes. It may be the greatest feat your mind has ever accomplished. The entire floor isn't as you would see things, but as he does."

Normally, when Christian watched videos inside his mansion, he did it from his own point of view. Seeing the world as an independent observer. Here, he could do both. He was still an observer, but by viewing the wall, he saw himself as Luke had.

Words shot out from the screen, projecting a hologram directly in front of Christian.

Intelligent, but he's little more than a boy.

Christian knew enough to understand they were Luke's thoughts.

"How accurate are they?" he said. "How well has my mind replicated what he thinks?"

"The best it could do, I imagine. I wasn't privy to it. You somehow built this and didn't allow me in."

"Then how do you know more than me?"

"It's been open for a few days. Since your dream," the Other said.

Christian nodded and walked forward. He heard the Other following him, although he kept a distance that he didn't usually respect.

As he went farther onto the floor, he realized the vast openness was divided into a trail of sorts. Statues stood on his left and walls to his right, creating a path. Christian came to a statue of Bradley Brown. It appeared extremely lifelike, the clothing and skin looking perfect.

Christian thought it was a statue, until it *moved.*

It was another projection. Brown turned to Christian and looked at him with sad eyes.

"Did Luke have something to do with you?" Christian asked.

Brown raised his hand and pointed at the wall behind Christian. Christian turned and saw another meeting between himself and Luke, one that had taken place in Luke's house late at night.

Christian saw himself pacing across the living room as he so often did through Luke's eyes.

He heard the words they spoke, but Luke's thoughts flew from the screen, capturing Christian's attention.

Perhaps I've been waiting for someone like him.

Christian watched the conversation take place and kept reading the thoughts popping from the screen.

When he'd had enough, he walked forward again, moving deeper into the maze. Veronica was next. Luke sat across from her outside a restaurant. Christian listened to the drink order and watched the conversation unfold.

You shouldn't have kept asking questions, Ms. Lopez, Luke's thoughts emanated from the wall. *You should have maintained your role as the gushing biographer.*

Christian kept walking, until he saw himself lying in Bradley Brown's living room. This was the first video not shown from Luke's point of view, but rather Brown's.

Four people besides Brown were in the room, all of

them bound in different places. Christian was on the floor. Tommy near him. Veronica was on the couch, and Charles Ranger—the crippled mute Bradley Brown cared for at the nursing home—was in his wheelchair.

Everything I need. All right here. The words hung in the air a foot from Christian's face. They weren't Luke's thoughts, but Brown's. *He gave it all to me.*

"No," Christian said aloud, his own words somehow scattering the ones that hung in the air. The video in front of him went black, as did all of the walls. "No. Luke didn't do that. I'm going insane and this is the byproduct."

"I wish that was the case," the Other said. "I really do. Our marriage was important for my survival."

The floor was silent for a few seconds, then the wall lit up again—the rest of them remaining black. Christian looked at John Presley's living room through someone else's eyes. He knew whose eyes, and he saw what the person had done. The woman lying on the floor was Mrs. Presley. Her fingers were detached and discarded, blood spurting across the gray carpet from her hands.

Christian shook his head. *No.*

He watched as the man knelt and took out the woman's eyes. Surgically precise.

Then he heard the person speak, the face turning its attention to John Presley, who was tied up on the couch.

Luke's voice filled the entire floor, booming like a god.

Christian looked up at the ceiling, desperately wanting to find Luke's eyes. They still stared at him.

"Keep going," the Other said. "There's more. A *lot* more."

As Christian moved through his mind's vast replication

of his and Luke's relationship, he realized there might be more here than he could view in an entire lifetime.

———

Christian opened his eyes. The rug that had no place in this house. He pulled his phone out and looked at the time. He had an hour left, but he knew it wasn't enough. If everything he'd just seen were true, if even a fraction of it turned out to be right, then a lot of people were very close to dying, and not at Ted Hinson's hands.

He called Tommy's phone.

"Are you finished?" Tommy answered.

"Has Luke called you?"

"No? Now answer my question."

"Listen to me, Tommy. Everyone's life depends on it. Do *not* contact him and do *not* answer his calls. Go back to the office and wait there—"

"No. Fuck you. I'm not doing it. I'm going into that house, Christian, and I don't care what else you say to me."

"*Please!*" Christian shouted.

Tommy said nothing, letting silence take over. Rage and despair dominated Christian's plea, and Tommy had to hear it. Rage at Luke. Despair at how far off they all were.

Christian swallowed, and when he spoke, his voice was just above a whisper. "I need two more hours. That's it. The next time I call you, I'll know everything, okay? Just two hours. You were already going to give me one more."

Tommy said nothing for thirty seconds. "Fine. Two hours, Christian, and not another second more."

"Thank you," Christian told him, but the call went dead before Tommy heard it.

Christian didn't wait to think. He stood from the couch and left the house.

He had one more stop, and there he'd either confirm what he saw in his mansion, or accept that he was going insane.

CHAPTER TWENTY-SIX

Luke had spent the last two hours contemplating what he'd seen at the FBI building: Christian's bright fear.

Two hours of thinking, and in the end the outcome was unavoidable. Luke rarely focused on a problem for long. His brain was usually able to come up with the solution quickly. This, however, was different, and it took longer.

He had sat in the back of the FBI car, passively listening to the small talk from the agents. But finally, his mind clicked home, and when it did, a calm truth lay across Luke.

Christian knew, and if he didn't yet, he would very shortly. Somehow, his mind had put everything together.

Luke looked at the agent sitting in the driver's seat. He stared at the man's neck.

Hadn't it always been a possibility that Christian would figure everything out? Certainly. The boy's ability to understand other people was without equal. Luke had held Christian at bay for so long because of the mental games he'd foisted on him. He had been creating more problems

—both physical and psychological—than Christian could deal with, and that had prevented him from seeing the truth.

Until now.

The fear was the tell. Christian had burned with terror. If he hadn't already, he was close to figuring everything out.

Luke didn't hesitate once he understood this new reality.

He grabbed the knife in his pocket and sliced the first agent's throat. Blood splashed against the windshield, his heart pumping at full blast. The other agent had time to turn his head before Luke opened his throat.

His blood coated the first agent's face and shoulder.

Luke pocketed the knife as the two gurgled in front, their hands desperately trying to somehow stem the pouring blood.

He stepped from the back of the vehicle and closed the door behind him. Blood covered his right hand, bright and warm. He didn't bother to wipe it off. He stood at the driver's door, watching as the two died inside.

Once they had expired, Luke opened the door and shoved the driver into the passenger's seat, putting him on top of his dead partner. He looked at the bloody seat and resigned himself to the fact that his suit was ruined. Blood was unavoidable at this point. He wasn't worried. He could still salvage this.

He'd need to act quickly, but hadn't this been what he always wanted? An all-out war with God?

So be it.

Luke sat in the front seat and pulled the car into

Hinson's driveway. He briefly considered the options available to him. He couldn't dump them inside the house. That was too risky. He'd have to discard the bodies after everything was finished. Luke needed to get to Hinson. He'd let his subconscious mind determine a solution for the two agents while he busied himself with the present.

———

Tommy was in his office. The computer screen in front of him was blank, though he kept staring at it. He had already called Vadik twice to see if there was any new information, annoying the cop.

Vadik had finally said in a tone that would have angered Tommy if he didn't know the man was right, "*I* will call *you* when I have something new."

Do not contact Luke, Christian had told him. That was all Tommy wanted to do.

Well, not *all*, but if he wasn't going to rush into Mackenrow's house, then that was his next instinct.

Tommy had spent the past few hours frantic. Christian's last call had put him into a near frenzy. Now was the first time since leaving Mackenrow's home that he was able to calm down slightly, which gave him time to consider Christian's directive. Before, he had only focused on the fact that he had to *wait*.

But Christian had said more than that. He'd said that Tommy shouldn't call Luke.

Why? Luke was as much a part of this as Christian. Perhaps more so, given Luke's extensive experience. Luke hadn't radically changed the past year.

Fuck that, Tommy thought. *If Christian is going to keep me here while he explores his mind, or whatever the hell he's doing, then I'm going to see what Luke thinks.*

Tommy was going into that house, regardless of the consequences, but he'd prefer to have backup.

He picked up his cellphone and found Luke's number.

"Hello," Luke answered.

"Hey. Look, I need to talk to you. Do you have a second?"

"Sure. I'm just sitting in the back of a car staring at a house."

Tommy sighed, not sure where to begin. Everything that had happened felt jumbled in his mind, like a pile of wires. "Okay. We went to Mackenrow's house and things are definitely not right there. They're fucked, Luke. That's the best way to put it. The woman was near tears, but she told us she didn't have time to talk about her husband because she *had to go to work.* We told her that she *and* her daughter were in danger, but that didn't faze her a bit. She shut the door in our face. The guy is over there, Luke, and he's holding them hostage."

"Where are you now?"

"I'm at the office." Tommy said.

"Why?"

"That's the other part. We leave the house and get in the car, then Christian says he needs three hours before we can do anything. He said I shouldn't call you or answer your calls, either."

"Why would he say that?" Luke asked.

"Fuck if I know. Look, I want to go into that house right now. I don't want to go in with other agents, though."

Tommy closed his eyes, knowing what he was about to ask his partner. "I'm going to break pretty much everything in the search and seizure amendment, but I'm fine with it. If you come with me, you'll be doing the same. I *know* what I'm asking isn't right, and I know what it could mean for your life, but I don't have anyone else to ask."

Tommy listened to the phone's silence, his heart thumping in his chest as if he'd smoked meth. He wanted Luke with him. They'd been partners for years.

"I'm going regardless," Tommy said. "Now. I'm not waiting on Christian anymore. The kid has snapped, I think. If I have to go alone, that's fine, but—"

"Meet me at the house," Luke said. "I'll be there in twenty minutes."

Luke ended the phone call and placed the phone on the dining room table. Three people sat around the table. Mr. Hinson, Ms. Mackenrow, and their young daughter, Callie. He smiled at them. The adults looked at him, but their daughter stared at the fourth person—well, body—occupying the table.

Alice sat at the head, her destroyed head still slumped on her chest.

"Honey," the mother whispered. "Look at me, okay? Don't look at that."

Ms. Mackenrow was doing everything in her power to remain composed, and Luke admired that. Composure under stress was severely lacking in this modern world. People panicked over missing a turn because their GPS lagged a few seconds. Silliness, when four thousand years ago humans had been competing with animal predators for survival.

Dr. Hinson wasn't holding up nearly as well. He looked at Luke, which was better than completely collapsing, but a steady stream of tears were running down his face.

"Okay," Luke said. "There has been a change of plan, but these things are necessary when dealing with so many moving parts. I hope you understand."

He looked directly at Ted Hinson.

"Dr. Hinson, I need you to pay attention to me right now. Can you do that?"

Hinson nodded. The man had looked so composed when Luke had met him in that DC nightclub. No longer. The love-obsessed parasite was now a frightened lamb. Perhaps *that* was giving him too much credit. Hinson was an insect, only knowing its habitat was collapsing around it.

"Okay. Now watch closely."

Luke's pistol flashed up, moving like a gunslinger of old. The suppressed barrel fired two bullets, one entering the woman's and other the girl's head.

The suppressor muffled the sound and the bullets' velocity, and the subsonic ammo did not exit their skulls. Blood leaked down the front of their faces from the small black holes sitting in the middles of their foreheads.

They stared emptily forward for a long moment. Then the mother fell backward, slumping down in her chair. The daughter fell forward, her head landing with a wet *smack* on the wooden table.

Hinson shrieked, a high, girlish sound.

Luke silenced him with a look. "Good. You saw that. I didn't want you to miss it. Now, there's still a chance you make it out of here alive, but that depends on you. Go sit in the living room. A man is coming over. When he enters the house, I want you to stare straight ahead, no matter what happens. Don't look at him and don't say anything. Just stare ahead, okay?"

CHAPTER TWENTY-SEVEN

"Mr. Ranger, my name is Christian Windsor. Do you remember me?"

The old man sat in his wheelchair, his eyes wide and his face nearly the color of copy paper. Everyone else Bradley Brown had captured knew only Luke's version of events. This might be the single man who knew differently.

On the way here, Christian had driven thirty over the speed limit, rushing as an all-consuming need to hear the truth filled him. Christian had flashed his FBI ID at a few nurses and got a pretty quick meeting with Charles Ranger.

"Sir, do you remember me?" Christian asked again.

The man looked paralyzed with fear. He nodded, but just barely.

"Good. I was there with you that night, the one with Bradley Brown. You remember that too, right?" Christian didn't know how much Ranger's mind had deteriorated over the intervening years. He had been fully functional back then, if mute and crippled, but time changed everyone. Christian knew that only too well.

Ranger again nodded.

"You're not in trouble, sir. You may be the only person who can save a lot of lives so it's important that you answer me truthfully. I promise, whatever you say to me, I'm going to protect you." Christian leaned forward in his chair. "What I'm saying is, as long as I'm alive, nothing bad will happen to you, okay?"

The man didn't move. His eyes were watering and his lower lip quivering. Christian had to ask now, before Ranger broke completely.

"That night, in Brown's house, did Luke Titan have anything to do with it? Did he help Brown at all?"

A tear fell from the man's eye and onto his wrinkled, pale face. His lip kept quivering, but he didn't move. Seconds passed, perhaps a full minute, but Christian didn't budge. He held the man's stare in a way that he'd never done before in his life.

The man nodded. Christian stared for a few more seconds, but Ranger didn't stop. His head kept going up and down, at first hardly moving, then more vigorously.

"I'll be back." Christian stood and flew from the room.

He glanced back once before exiting. The old man was still nodding.

Tommy saw the unmarked FBI car parked farther down the neighborhood road. Luke had parked at least a hundred yards away. Tommy parked next to the curb and pulled his phone out.

"Where are you?" he asked when Luke answered.

"I'm inside. I… You need to see this," Luke said.

"Is she in there?" Tommy's hands shook, but he didn't exit the car. He could barely hold the phone to his ear, but he had to hear the answer before he went inside. He needed to know what he would see.

"No. Get in here, Tommy. Now."

Tommy hung the phone up and dropped it onto the seat. He got out of the car, unholstered his weapon, and ran across the yard. He paused for a second as he reached the stoop, positioning the pistol so that he was ready to fire.

He opened the door and saw the same small foyer from earlier this morning.

"Luke!"

"I'm in the bedroom."

Tommy walked into the living room, his weapon still raised.

Ted Hinson was sitting on the couch. He was shaking worse than Tommy had been in the car. Tears streamed down his face, and his eyes were red and swollen. Tommy stepped into the room, forgetting about Luke.

"Where is she?" Tommy said. "Where's Alice?"

The man's whole body started *shuddering*, as if he was caught in the middle of a blizzard. Tommy took another step forward, both anger and fear rising in him, twirling like thick threads braiding with one another as they moved from his gut to his head.

"*Where's my goddamn fiancée?*" he screamed, spit flying from his mouth.

Tommy heard nothing until the last footfall moved behind him. He felt something in the center of his neck, a single brilliant flash of pain that was gone as quickly as it had occurred.

He tried to turn, but found he couldn't move.

Tommy collapsed to the floor, his body losing all ability to function. He tried to get up, to roll over, to do *anything*, but his body wouldn't respond.

He lay unmoving on his side with only his eyes obeying his commands.

Luke walked into his field of vision. Tommy saw the ice pick hanging from his hand.

"Hey, partner," Luke said.

Tommy tried to speak, but only managed to leak spit from his lips. It slid down the side of his face.

"I want to show you something," Luke said. He reached down and grabbed Tommy's arms. He pulled him deeper into the living room,

Tommy's body flopped like a rag doll as Luke turned him over onto his back. He felt nothing; not Luke's grip nor the floor beneath him.

I'm paralyzed, he thought almost calmly. *Luke stabbed me and now I'm paralyzed.*

Luke dropped Tommy's arms and they remained lying above his head. He reached down and turned Tommy's face so that he was staring at Ted Hinson. "Beyond Mr. Hinson, there's a dining room. Can you see it?"

Tommy focused and saw what Luke was talking about. A small girl lay with her head on the table, and Christy Mackenrow was slumped in a chair with blood covering her face.

"To the left," Luke said.

Tommy's eyes moved slightly to the left and landed on Alice. The back of her head was a mess of destruction.

"I think you see it, Tommy. Good. Now we wait for Christian."

Christian dialed Tommy's number twenty times before giving up and throwing his phone across the car. It crashed against the window, bouncing off and hitting the seat next to him.

His car was reaching its limit in terms of speed. The speedometer read 130, and although he had the pedal pressed to the floor, the needle wasn't moving.

Christian's mind flashed through possibilities, but he shoved them away. He only had one thing to consider now. Should he call for backup? Either Tommy had gone into Mackenrow's home and done something he needed to clean up, or Luke had gotten hold of him.

Yet, if Tommy *had* killed Hinson, then he'd answer the phone, which he wasn't doing, and that left only one other option. Luke had him.

The phone rang. The car swerved dangerously as Christian reached for it. He put the phone to his ear without looking at the caller ID.

"Tommy?"

"No," Luke said. "Tommy's here, but he's unable to use the phone right now."

"Why?" Christian said, tears pricking his eyes like hot needles.

"We'll discuss all of that very soon. Come over to Ms. Mackenrow's. Call the other FBI agents and tell them to keep away from it. I'm sure you can think of a reason."

Christian burned with rage so hot he thought his skin might melt the phone.

"Christian, don't bring anyone else. Enough people have died. Let's not make an undertaker rich today."

The phone line went dead. Christian let it drop and it tumbled to his lap. He brought both hands to the steering wheel, gripping it until his hands were white.

He should call for backup. He had to, regardless of what Luke said. He knew that was the smart move. He glanced in the rearview mirror. His mother sat in the backseat beside Melissa.

When Christian looked to his right, he saw the Other with blood streaming down his face. His mother and Melissa looked at him through the rearview mirror, but the Other only stared ahead.

"He'll kill you if you don't call someone, honey," his mom said.

"You need to think with your head, not your emotions," Melissa said.

"Luke tried to kill everyone you love. He's played you and Tommy for fools, and wrecked your life. You may not be able to kill Hinson, but you *can* kill Luke," the Other said. "*If* you go alone. If not, someone else will get him… Or, they'll arrest him."

Christian gripped the steering wheel harder and continued racing down the highway.

CHAPTER TWENTY-EIGHT

This was a mess, no doubt about it. God had played His hand well, but Luke still had better cards. You can play a hand great, but if the other player knew what he was doing, you couldn't beat a great hand.

Tommy lay on the couch. Luke had stemmed the blood flow, which wasn't bad to begin with. Luke's medical doctorate was paying dividends in ways his professors probably never imagined. He had placed the ice pick perfectly, severing Tommy's spinal cord without doing any real internal damage.

Luke had moved the three dead bodies into a semicircle around the couch, each occupying a dining room chair.

Alice had the middle seat, right where Tommy could see her. After rearranging everyone in the living room, he had gone outside and moved his vehicle, ensuring that someone would have to walk up the driveway to see the bodies.

Luke stood at the living room window. The blinds were half open, his body shielding what lay inside.

It was all a mess, indeed.

Everything would be finished soon. Luke was beginning to think God might have a slight win here. Not 100%, but a moral victory, nonetheless.

There were too many bodies, and calls would be made soon. Perhaps not by anyone in this room, or even Christian, but Waverly? The director would be checking in, and when he couldn't get hold of anyone? That would be a problem.

Still, maybe it was salvageable. Everyone in here would need to die. Luke had no qualms about that. His qualms were with Christian's death. Luke didn't want him to die anymore, but it might be unavoidable.

He had set upon this endeavor with a specific goal in mind, and if Christian died today, Luke could continue his FBI rise, but his main goal wouldn't be accomplished.

Plus, there was Veronica Lopez to consider. If Luke killed everyone else off, she would be left. Veronica would suffer greatly from Christian's loss, but that wasn't her punishment. Hers had to be death.

Luke's jaw muscles flexed as he bit down. This battle was not with God, but himself. It was time to decide what he wanted in the long term.

***

Christian parked the car right next to the curb. There were too many vehicles in the driveway, including an undercover car from the FBI.

He stepped out of the car and walked across the street to Tommy's car. He looked in the windows but saw nothing. He took his weapon out and held it next to his leg, then looked over the car's hood at the house.

The blinds were partly open and Luke was standing at the window. His face was…different. No smile. Not even his usual calm.

He's concentrating.

Christian didn't raise his weapon at Luke. He wasn't a good enough shot to hit him from this distance, and if he missed Luke would move quickly to kill whoever was alive.

He walked up the driveway. As he passed the FBI cruiser, he saw two bodies lying across the back seat. Agents that had been sent to save Alice. Their throats were cut and blood covered the interior.

Christian wasn't surprised that Luke had driven it here in that condition. In Luke's mind, nothing could touch him.

His mother spoke from behind him, sounding calm as she always did. "Maybe nothing can, honey. Maybe you should get back in your car and call for backup."

He said nothing to the vision and continued walking up the driveway.

The door was open and he stepped inside, closing it behind him. He felt no panic or fear. No hope, either. Perhaps that's what serenity was, a lack of emotion.

I'm going to die today, he thought. *By a hand that I once loved.*

"In here, Christian," Luke said.

He walked across the foyer to the living room. He saw Tommy lying across the couch on his stomach, although much of him was blocked by the three bodies sitting around him.

Bodies. That's what they are, because people *are alive, and they're not.*

He looked around the room and he saw Ted Hinson sitting by the fireplace. He wasn't bound. His mouth wasn't even taped. His arms were wrapped around his knees, which were folded to his chest, and he rocked back and forth as he stared down at the carpet. Tears had been running down his face—his red eyes and salt stained cheeks spoke that loudly enough—but the tears had stopped.

A shell, Christian thought. *That's all he ever was. That's what you were willing to go to prison for. A shell of a human being, little more than the bodies to your left.*

No, another piece of him responded. *You were going to kill him to keep anyone else from dying.*

Maybe. Christian didn't know anymore. He turned to face Luke.

"I imagine this is a bit shocking for you," his partner said. "I'd like to have a palaver before we close this chapter on our lives, if that's okay with you?"

Christian's hands shook, and the gun at his side shook with it. He could level his weapon and fire, but what were the chances he'd hit anything besides a wall, even this close? It would be like someone with Parkinson's trying to shoot.

"I'd ask Tommy to join us, but he's not able to move." Luke didn't look at Tommy.

Christian did. Tommy stared back at him, rage alight in his eyes like a bright, red fire.

"Yes, he's very upset, but there's not much he can do

about it," Luke said. "I know you're upset, too, but you can still act on those emotions. It's a gift, isn't it?"

He met Luke's eyes.

"The kitchen?" Luke asked.

Christian instinctively backed up when Luke walked toward him.

Luke paused at the entrance, then turned. "Sorry, I forgot something."

He went back into the living room, passing by Christian again. He unholstered his weapon leisurely. Ted Hinson didn't look up.

Luke squeezed the trigger and Hinson's head painted the fireplace red and gray. "There."

He set the gun down neatly on the brick next to Hinson's fallen body. "I've unarmed myself. I don't expect you to do the same."

He passed Christian once again and entered the kitchen.

Christian looked at Tommy. He nodded, hoping the message was clear: *I'll kill him. For everything he did.*

He looked down at his hands. They were shaking. He closed his eyes and swallowed. He had to get control of himself if he was going to make good on that silent promise. He had to be able to aim and fire his damned weapon.

Christian opened his eyes and followed Luke into the kitchen.

Luke was leaning against the sink, as he'd done so many times in his own house. "I could make coffee, but this may not be the best time. I don't want my back to you." He smiled. It looked sad, as if he was sorry for everything that had happened.

No. He's sorry that it all has to end.

"You can kill me now, or we can talk. You can trust I will be truthful. I have always been so with you. I know you think I've lied, and probably would point to the living room as evidence. I didn't lie, Christian. You just refused to *see*. However, I'll speak plainly, starting with this. Your best chance of leaving here alive is to kill me now. If you wait, your chances decrease."

Christian didn't believe that whatsoever. His hands hadn't settled yet, but they would. His shaking hands weren't all that kept him from raising his pistol.

He wanted to hear what Luke had to say.

Haven't you always? Haven't his words held you in a trance since the moment you met him? His intelligence rivals your own, and in that, you thought you found kin.

"Why?" Christian asked, his lips barely moving.

Luke gave a single, silent laugh, his chest hitching. He looked down at his feet, as if he was totally in control of the situation. He didn't care that Christian held a pistol and he had nothing but a bloody, three-piece suit.

"I told you I believe in God. I understand His purpose, Christian." Luke didn't look up from his leather shoes. "It is order. Everything in the universe is constantly trying to create disorder. Stars exploding, asteroids colliding with planets. The very fact of the universe's continual expansion shows its defiance of His will. Death and disorder is the way of the universe. God prefers life and order."

Luke looked up at last. His brown eyes were as hard as sunbaked brick. "Life for some. Death for others. But death is on *His* terms, not our own."

He walked over to the kitchen window and pulled the

blinds up, letting in sunlight. It cast his shadow dark behind him.

"The people I was accused of killing by Veronica all died at my hands. They served a greater purpose. My purpose. That purpose is simple, to create more disorder in this world than any human ever has." He turned, the sunlight casting his face in semi-darkness.

Christian didn't know that purpose could be personified, but he saw it in the man before him.

"You are a tool in that disorder," Luke continued. "The creation of it. I'm not sure I could have met a more perfectly shaped tool than you, Christian. But things have changed, and I must recognize that. You won't be let loose in the same way that I had hoped, but all is not lost. Indeed, the room behind you is full of disorder, and God certainly finds it an affront."

"You're insane," Christian said.

Luke laughed, a deep one that came from his stomach and filled the room. It would have been pleasant if not for the blood soaking his clothes. Instead, it was horrific.

He spoke when his laughter died, although the smile remained on his face. "Insanity is praying to a being, wishing that he would look after you when it's clear he doesn't care in the slightest. The order God wants is only *His* order, while the universe wishes for something completely different. He rules this world like a tyrant and people beg at His table for crumbs."

Luke's voice changed into that of a mocking child. "Please, sir, help me pay this bill. Please, Lord, let me make it to work on time. God, will you please help me find my car keys?"

He laughed again, and Christian knew it to be real, not a facade. He found the prayers of desperate people humorous.

"It's a joke. The greatest thing humanity could do would be to reject God, and do everything in its power to create the disorder he holds such disdain for."

"Tommy…" Christian shook his head in sorrow. His next words were a whisper. "Tommy is paralyzed, and you're saying it's to get back at God? Do you understand that's crazier than anything we've come across? You're mad, Luke. Helplessly insane."

"This is the first step on your path to enlightenment. You first must hear the word before you can understand it."

Christian looked up. "What did you expect from me? To turn into a serial killer?"

Luke shrugged. "At first, no. At first, I thought you would die after having committed some horrible actions. I changed my mind the more I got to know you. A serial killer? Perhaps, but that would have been a side effect. No, you were to be a growing cancer inside the FBI. Tommy and I would have helped. Covering up your misdeeds. Eventually, someone would catch on, or Tommy wouldn't have been able to take it anymore. Then your mind would have had to create more disorder."

"That's nothing, Luke. Even in your crazy fucking scheme, that's not disorder on the scale of a Hitler or Stalin."

Luke spat on the floor. "Hitler? Stalin? They served themselves and whatever other delusions they held. *My* disorder is a direct assault on God, with *purpose*. He knows it and He's fighting it, which is why you understood what I had done before *I* was ready for you to know."

"You think God influenced this?" Christian shook his head, unable to believe anything coming from Luke.

"You're here, aren't you? Just in the nick of time."

Christian couldn't take anymore. Luke was crazy, and his intelligence had masked it for far too long. It was time to end this. He raised his weapon. "You're under arrest. Turn around and put your hands behind your head."

Luke smiled. "Christian, this is your last chance. Kill me now."

"Turn around. Put your hands behind your head."

"As you wish." Luke turned and looked out of the window. He raised his hands to the back of his head and put them together.

"Get on your knees," Christian said.

Luke complied, elegantly lowering himself to the floor.

Christian pulled the cuffs from the small holding pouch on his belt. He clicked the buttons with his left hand, allowing them to fall open. He walked across the kitchen toward Luke. "My gun is aimed directly at your head. Don't move."

"Why not kill me, Christian?"

"We'll see how much disorder you can sow in prison. Or in the electric chair."

Christian stood behind his former partner, who knelt on the floor, surrendering after killing so many people. He held the weapon in his right hand and reached for Luke's left. He grabbed it firmly, the shaking banished. He twisted Luke's arm, bringing it down behind his back. He went for the right hand next.

Did you ever think you were in control? his mind wondered as Luke spun. *Did you believe that you could beat him?*

The words flashed through his mind, which was reading everything around him as it always had. He couldn't react quickly enough, not even to pull the trigger.

Luke's right hand grabbed Christian's left as he turned his body. Everything moved nearly too fast for the eye to see. One second, Luke was on the floor, and the next, Christian's face slammed against the window.

He fired the gun and a bullet blasted through the ceiling. Small white specks floated down around them. A hot explosion of pain burst in Christian's wrist and rippled up his arm. The pistol fell to the floor.

He felt Luke's breath in his ear. He could smell the blood on Luke's suit, all of it so close. One of Christian's arms was twisted painfully behind him, his broken wrist trapped against the window.

"Never forget that I gave you a chance to kill me. Multiple chances," Luke whispered, his breath brushing Christian's face. "Disorder, Christian. You and I, we're going to create a lot of it."

The pain in Christian's wrist subsided significantly when the knife entered his side. Luke stuck it deep and dragged it upward, from the top of his hip to the bottom of his rib cage.

Christian felt Luke pull the knife out, then indescribable pain ripped through his head and he felt hot blood running down his cheek.

"See you soon, Christian."

Gray preceded black, and Christian knew nothing else.

CHAPTER TWENTY-NINE

They took the living first. Then the dead were removed from the house one by one. Waverly stood watching over it all, asking questions of himself for which there were no answers.

He watched the paramedics wheel Tommy to the ambulance. Tommy didn't look at him as he passed. He watched the medics attend to Christian in the kitchen, trying to close the wounds and stabilize him. A knife handle stuck out from his face, the blade dug deep inside his head.

A short time later, Waverly watched them wheel his second FBI agent out on a stretcher. He went back into the house and gazed at the four bodies in the living room.

There was no need to search for the perpetrator. Luke Titan had called it in himself.

Waverly's fists clenched as he remembered the call that had come in as the FBI jet streaked from DC to Atlanta.

"Director, it's Luke Titan."

"I was just about to call you. I tried Tommy but got nothing. Same with Christian."

"That's understandable. They're both tremendously injured. I don't think Tommy will die, but Christian might."

"What are you talking about?"

"I stabbed Tommy in the neck, paralyzing him. Then I gutted Christian before shoving the knife into his face. He's bleeding heavily."

Waverly was stunned, unable to speak.

"They're all at Christy Mackenrow's house. You should have the address, or one of your underlings will. I'm heading out, Director Waverly. I do think we'll meet again. There's that to look forward to, at least."

The phone line had gone dead. Waverly usually acted quickly on new information, but not then. He hadn't lowered the phone from his ear, too stunned to do more than stare into the near distance for a long moment.

It had taken him a solid minute to realize he still hadn't put down his phone.

When he'd come to his senses, he'd called everyone he had available to the Mackenrow house and issued an all-points bulletin for Luke Titan. He'd landed in Atlanta and gone directly to the house, wanting to see the truth for himself.

Waverly had scheduled a press conference for within the hour, and it would run on every news network for the next two days. Ten minutes ago, his agents had broken down the locked door to Ted Hinson's basement and found two women alive and chained to a wall.

The other missing women were chained as well, but they were dead. The surviving women were in shock, unable to talk, but that was very distant in Waverly's mind. He was looking at the person who committed those crimes, slumped dead against the fireplace.

No, coldly, he wasn't as concerned about *those* victims.

There was much to do, but Waverly couldn't pull himself from the disaster surrounding him. He didn't understand how any of it had happened, or why.

The dead are everywhere, he thought, *and it occurred on your watch.*

He looked away from the bloody living room and walked out onto the stoop. Agents passed by him, saying nothing. Both his presence and the body count kept them silent.

Luke Titan had done this. Luke Titan had paralyzed one partner, and may have killed another. The paramedics had said Christian was in critical condition, and when Waverly asked, they'd put his survival at fifty percent.

Waverly had to find Luke before the man left the country.

CHAPTER THIRTY

Christian was in a coma for a week and a half before regaining consciousness. The doctors let his mother and Veronica visit, but only for a few minutes.

"We haven't left and we're not going to," Veronica had said. His mother couldn't talk, but she cried and touched him gently.

Nurses rushed them out, and Christian had fallen asleep.

He had dreamed that he and Luke were in a car, a convertible. The top was down and they were rolling along an empty stretch of highway somewhere out west. The desert surrounded them, with tan rock mountains rising in the distance. The wind filled the car, tossing their hair constantly.

Luke was smiling at Christian. His eyes were alive, full of excitement. Christian glanced at the speedometer and saw they were moving at close to 150.

"We're going to have fun, Christian. So very much fun."

Christian turned his head and looked ahead.

If he dreamed anything else, he didn't remember. When he woke, his doctor was waiting to speak to him.

"We're loosening the wires on your face. You'll be able to open your jaw just enough to speak, but only if you agree to us doing this." The doctor shook his head. "We don't think it's in your best interest, but your boss is insisting that he be able to interview you. The man is… persistent, to say the least."

Christian agreed to loosen the wiring. He wanted to speak with his mother and Veronica before Waverly.

"I keep ending up here," Christian mumbled. It was the first time he'd spoken in two weeks, though he came out of his coma a few days ago.

His mother stood at the side of Christian's hospital bed, tears streaming down her face. Veronica was on the other side, crying as well. Happiness and sadness filled both of them.

Christian hadn't requested a mirror to see his face since waking. He didn't need one. The sympathy and pain in his mother's eyes showed him everything.

He'd been given no information since awakening, and when he'd motioned for paper, his nurses had told him to rest and given him more sedatives. His head felt as if the flesh and bone had been rubbed for hours with sandpaper. Speaking made it feel like the sandpaper was back, and spunky.

"Tommy?" he whispered, hoping he didn't have to say more.

"He's alive," Veronica said.

His mother squeezed his hand. Christian pushed her

away and twirled two fingers in a forward circular motion. *Go on.*

"He's paralyzed. He was cleared for visitors two days ago, but he won't see anyone."

Christian twirled his fingers again. There was more, and she was holding back. "Recovery?" he managed to say.

"The doctors told us there would be some, but he'll never walk again." Tears filled Veronica's eyes again and she choked out the next sentence. "He'll be a quadriplegic, Christian. He may never speak again."

Christian closed his eyes and let his head fall deeper into the pillow.

"Waverly," he whispered.

Both of them took his unbroken wrist and kissed his hand, Veronica moving around the bed to do so. They left, and the director walked in a few minutes later.

The two stared at each other for half a minute, and Christian saw no sympathy or sadness in the man. He saw rage. Determination.

"The doctors don't want you speaking, as I'm sure they've told you. There's a risk you won't fully heal, and I want you to understand that up front. I pushed them until they agreed to ask, and the fact that I'm here shows you allowed them to loosen the contraption on your head. If you want to wait, tell me, and I'll leave. I won't be responsible for more damage to you."

"Do you...want...to wait?" Christian asked. Tears formed in his eyes at the pain from speaking.

"I'm here, aren't I?"

"Let's...talk, then," Christian said.

Waverly pulled a chair up to the bed and took out a

spiral notebook. He opened it to the first page and grabbed a pen from his shirt pocket. "Take your time. I'll go as long you can take, then you rest. I'll wait in the lobby. I'm not leaving the hospital until you tell me you're done. If that takes a month, so be it. I want the whole story."

Christian nodded and slowly started talking.

FOR CHRISTIAN WINDSOR

Address:

Emory University Hospital

Atlanta, GA 30322

Recipient:

Special Agent with the Federal Bureau of Investigation,
Christian Windsor

Dear Christian,

I've read that you survived. I must admit, that surprised me. To me, you were always a boy. Never a man. Perhaps your survival earns you that honor. I will no longer think of you as a boy, but as a man. Do you find some solace in that?

I wonder if Tommy is happy with what I did for him? His fiancée is dead (unfortunately, I couldn't attend her funeral), but he is still alive. That should certainly be considered a blessing.

Do you think he'll ever speak again? I must say, the insertion into his neck was very precise. I don't take pride in many of my accomplishments. To whom much is given, much is expected. But

I do in that bit of work. A millimeter difference, and he would have died. Instead, he has his life.

Waverly is doing his best to make things hard for me. He is a man possessed. I haven't spoken to him again, nor written him, but I imagine he wants to look me in the eye before he kills me. Or jails me. Please send him my regards, and tell him I will one day grant him that opportunity.

I wonder, Christian, is it winter where you are? I cannot imagine that you're seeing spring flowers bloom. I don't imagine you'll ever see them again. You might think killing me will birth a single rose. I promise, it won't.

Will you come for me, Christian? Will you come to do what you should have done in the kitchen?

I sacrificed a lot to create you. Think of it. Multiple careers, all landing me in the upper echelons of my colleagues. I would, without doubt, have landed there at the FBI, too. I gave it all up. For you. To ensure that you reached an endless winter.

I'm not done, Christian. In fact, I think I may just be starting. With sacrifice comes reward, and mine shall be great. Purpose drives me. It always has.

Now that you know my purpose, you may be able to anticipate some of my coming actions. Or, perhaps you're right and I'm insane. In that case, lunatics are notoriously unpredictable. If I were you, I would hope my purpose isn't crazy, but rational. It'll make catching me much easier.

Like I told you in the house, I'll see you soon.

I'll see all of you soon.

Yours,

Luke Titan, MD, PhD, Special Agent for the Federal Bureau of Investigations, Top Ten of America's Most Wanted

You're almost halfway finished with Luke's madness. Find out what happens next in *The General's Weapon.*

PREVIEW OF THE GENERAL'S WEAPON

The sun shone with such ferocity that it seemed to be taking revenge on the small Venezuelan town for some slight that no one could quite remember.

At one in the afternoon, the streets were nearly empty because the people couldn't handle the heat. Even the dogs knew it was smarter to seek shade than to venture out looking for scraps.

Christian Windsor sat in the back of an unmarked van with his sweat soaking through his shirt. The van's air conditioning couldn't keep up. He kept having to wipe his forehead, and had already downed two bottles of water in the past hour.

There were four vans in total, two on the block opposite of Christian's, and another sitting in front of him. He wondered if it was too many, but the local authorities had promised that the vans were nothing out of the ordinary. They all looked worn out. Christian's was almost broken.

He had stared out the front window as they drove, and

saw the Venezuelan police hadn't been exaggerating. Destroyed vans littered the city.

Christian didn't know for certain that Luke Titan was less than five hundred yards from him, but the probability was high. He had done something similar to this three other times in the past eighteen months, and each time he'd come up empty handed. In all three instances, Christian had been right that Luke Titan was there. However, he'd been wrong on his timing.

Not this time. Luke's here, and you're going to get him.

"How much longer?" he asked.

There were six people in the back of the van, and a driver and passenger were up front. The people in front wore painter's overalls. Those in the back wore heavy, bullet-proof armor and all had multiple guns holstered around their bodies. Each held an automatic weapon on their lap, and none of the men appeared to have a single ounce of fat on them.

"Ten minutes," the man to Christian's right said.

He didn't know these people. They weren't with the FBI, but from other federal departments. Most likely the CIA, although Christian didn't concern himself with that. How these people had arrived here and where they came from was FBI Director Alan Waverly's job.

Christian's job was to capture Luke Titan.

The operation teams had ceased demanding that Christian remain in the States while their missions took place. Waverly had done a good job stating Christian's case and refusing their attempts to sideline him. He would be there when they either cuffed or killed Luke.

Christian used the towel on his lap to wipe the sweat from his brow. He wore the same tactical gear as those around him, although they hadn't equipped him with any automatic weapons. His pistol was strapped to his side. He'd practiced enough over the last year to pass as a decent shot.

The walkie-talkie sprang to life with a burst of static. "Bravo Team, come in, over."

"Bravo Team here, over," the man holding the walkie-talkie said.

"We have eyes on the target. He's crossing the street and heading to home base."

Christian stared at the bearded man next to him, desperately wanting to hear the words that would set the troops loose. The man didn't return his look.

"Copy. Distance? Over."

"Twenty feet, over."

The van pulled away from the curb. The person driving knew the plan of attack. Christian watched out the front window as they took a right.

Then he saw Luke.

Luke was wearing shorts and a light blue linen shirt. Flip-flops adorned his feet.

The van sped up and didn't pause for the curb, but jumped right onto it, causing everyone inside to bounce on the benches. Christian saw the other three vans moving in, flying across the street and jumping onto the apartment building's brown lawn.

"Subdue the target at all costs," the man to his right said into the walkie-talkie.

The van slammed to a stop and everyone piled out, every agent holding their automatic weapon in the ready position.

Christian stood as the last man jumped out, intent on following just as quickly, yet he paused. Luke had turned and was watching the men dispersing from the vans. His hands weren't raised, and even from Christian's current distance, he could see the smile on his ex-partner's face.

Luke's gaze scanned his surroundings and somehow, despite the thirty men surrounding him, landed on Christian. He raised his hand and gave a small wave.

Christian jumped from the van and rounded its corner with his pistol raised and focused on Luke.

"Christian," his ex-partner called across the dead lawn. "If I didn't know better, I would think you miss me. You seem to be constantly trying to find me."

"*Kneel the fuck down!*"

Christian didn't know who screamed the order at Luke. He wouldn't take his eyes off the fugitive to figure it out, either. In a year and a half, they had never been this close to him. This was the first time Christian had laid eyes on Luke outside of video recordings since he had gutted him and stabbed him through the face.

"Christian, why are you doing this to yourself?" Luke asked. He hadn't knelt, nor made any other movement. "I told you I would come for you, didn't I? I said I'd see you soon. That I'd see all of you soon. Why are you inviting me before the time is right?"

"*Get the fuck down!*" someone else screamed.

Christian wouldn't have believed what happened next if

he wasn't there. Had someone told him what Luke had done, he would have thought it a myth to build up Luke's legacy. Christian *was* there, though, and neither his eyes nor mind lied to him.

Someone was moving in on Luke's right, perhaps the person who had just screamed at him.

Luke's gaze flashed to him, while the rest of his body remained facing Christian. The fully-armored agent stopped dead in his tracks. The entire group was closing in on Luke, encircling him, but that man stopped moving, caught in Luke's stare. He paused as the rest of the group continued tightening the noose.

Luke looked back at Christian.

"Okay, then," he said. "Have it your way."

Christian was twenty yards out from where Luke was standing, while the rest of the team was maybe five yards away.

Luke took a step back and raised his hands in the air.

"*Do not move!*" the first agent screamed. "*Don't take another fucking step!*"

"I'm not resisting," Luke said, moving back another step.

Christian's body was entranced by Luke's stare, but his mind wasn't. It saw what no one else did.

Luke was retreating, but there wasn't anywhere for him to go. There was *another* reason for it.

"*No!*" Christian shouted, just as Luke's foot reached the stoop to his apartment. "*Get back!*"

The agents heard Christian and paused briefly, a few of them looking over their shoulders. Luke stepped onto the stoop and other agents started screaming. Christian had set off panic in them. They yelled at Luke to get down, to surrender, to do everything except what the fuck he *was* doing.

"Christian!" Luke shouted above the fray. "You did this!"

Christian's mind categorized everything that happened next, even though his eyes couldn't keep up as it occurred. It was only later that he would be able to replay it back with a writer's attention to detail. Everything perfectly in place as if he'd written the scene himself.

The yard exploded.

Christian watched as the dirt around the street sprayed outward, followed immediately by fire and crumbling concrete. The earth shook beneath him, as if cannons had been installed beneath the street and fired simultaneously. More flames erupted.

The men in front of Christian had no chance, and if he hadn't paused inside the van, he would have died as easily as they did. Their bodies were blown apart from the blasts, their limbs separating from their torsos like steamed chicken legs. Blood burst from ripped organs, coagulating with the dust in the air and creating a red, dirty mist.

Christian hit the ground and put his hands over his head, rolling onto his stomach as fire and shards of concrete rained down around him. He kept his eyes on Luke through the blood permeating the air and the destruction falling from the sky.

Shots were fired, ricocheting off the building behind him. Luke was somehow guarding Christian and saving him for a worse fate—nothing touched him.

The last explosion splattered dirt and body parts across

the ground. Christian tried to regain his feet, stumbling as he did and falling to a knee.

"Stop chasing me, Christian," Luke called. Christian could hardly hear his words through the ringing in his ears. "You'll have your chance soon enough."

Get it here! The General's Weapon

ON PURPOSE AND OTHER THINGS

Thanks for reading, and I mean that wholeheartedly. I love telling stories and without you, that wouldn't be possible.

I know at the end of books, a lot of writers offer you something free if you sign-up for their mailing list. What they're doing, essentially, is buying your email address.

I don't want to do that.

I think having a purpose in life is important. It adds clarity and meaning to what you do. I'm lucky to know mine and that purpose dictates my life: I'm here to tell stories. Nothing else even comes close to the happiness this job gives me.

With that said, if you like reading my novels and want to know when the next book comes out, sign-up below. No tricks. No buying your address. Just me telling stories and you enjoying them.

The way these relationships should work.

Join Here:
https://www.subscribepage.com/danielscott

CONNECT WITH THE AUTHOR

Join Daniel's Email List here:

https://www.subscribepage.com/danielscott

9 7 9 8 8 8 5 4 1 9 4 7 5